Praise for the novels of John Lescroart

The Oath

A *People* Page-Turner

"A particularly strong plot."—*Los Angeles Times*

"Topical and full of intrigue."—*Milwaukee Journal Sentinel*

"Gripping, timely, and extremely satisfying."—*Booklist*

"Lescroart skillfully balances his story, blending the action of the plot with the satisfying details of Hardy's and Glitsky's personal lives. The minutiae of marriages, children, and domestic routines not only round out the characters but provide a smart counterpoint to the cops-and-lawyer stuff. And unlike so many other authors, Lescroart handles social commentary with a deft touch." *The Cleveland Plain Dealer*

The Hearing

"A spine-tingling legal thriller."—Larry King, *USA Today*

"Highly entertaining."—*Chicago Tribune*

"Excellent stuff."—*San Jose Mercury News*

continued . . .

Nothing But the Truth

"The novel's pacing is reminiscent of classic Ross MacDonald, where a week's worth of events is condensed into a few hours . . . a winning thriller."
—*Publishers Weekly* (starred review)

"Riveting . . . one of Lescroart's best tales yet."
—*Chicago Tribune*

"A rousing courtroom showdown."
—*Kirkus Reviews* (starred review)

The Mercy Rule

"A thought-provoking and important novel. . . . Well written, well plotted, well done."—Nelson DeMille

"Readers of *The 13th Juror* will already be off reading this book, not this review. Join them."—*The Philadelphia Inquirer*

JOHN LESCROART

■

SON OF HOLMES

NEW AMERICAN LIBRARY

NEW AMERICAN LIBRARY
Published by New American Library, a division of
Penguin Group (USA) Inc., 375 Hudson Street,
New York, New York 10014, U.S.A.
Penguin Books Ltd, 80 Strand, London WC2R 0RL, England
Penguin Books Australia Ltd, 250 Camberwell Road,
Camberwell, Victoria 3124, Australia
Penguin Books Canada Ltd, 10 Alcorn Avenue,
Toronto, Ontario, Canada M4V 3B2
Penguin Books (N.Z.) Ltd, Cnr Rosedale and Airborne Roads,
Albany, Auckland 1310, New Zealand

Penguin Books Ltd, Registered Offices: 80 Strand, London WC2R 0RL, England

Published by New American Library, an imprint of New American Library, a division
of Penguin Group (USA) Inc. Previously published in hardcover and trade paperback
editions by Donald I. Fine, Inc. For information address Penguin Group (USA) Inc.,
375 Hudson Street, New York, New York 10014.

First New American Library Printing, September 2003
3   5   7   9   8   6   4   2

 REGISTERED TRADEMARK—MARCA REGISTRADA

Set in Bembo
Printed in the United States of America

PUBLISHER'S NOTE
This is a work of fiction. Names, characters, places, and incidents either are the product
of the author's imagination or are used fictitiously, and any resemblance to actual persons, living or dead, business establishments, events, or locales is entirely coincidental.

For Lisa

PREFACE

All the events in this book are true, despite the disclaimer which you have just read if you read a book from cover to cover. A certain concession has been made so that living persons involved may not be subjected to inconvenience, scrutiny, or unwanted harassment. Nevertheless, no names have been changed, no places altered. The concession has been the disclaimer, which will convince most of the public that even this preface is fiction, though this is not the case.

PROLOGUE

The Martha Hudson dinner had been set for the sixth of January. To followers of the Master, Sherlock Holmes, this date is as important a day as the year offers, for on January 6, Holmes's birthday, his followers from all corners of the globe gather to celebrate his genius. On this date in 1983, I was invited to the Hudson dinner in Arlington, Massachusetts.

At the time, I was living in rather cramped quarters in Cambridge, and a free dinner meant much more to me than intellectual stimulation. I hadn't read many detective stories and knew little about them. However, I'd naturally heard about Holmes and thought the night might prove interesting.

It was bitter cold and snowing—the wet, slushy snow of the city—when I left my apartment wrapped in an old army coat. The suit I had borrowed for the affair was ill-fitting, and I waited in great discomfort for the bus out of Harvard Square. The ride to Arlington took nearly forty-five minutes, and I kept asking myself as I shivered if all this was worth a free meal.

For the past several months, I had been trying and failing to make my living as a songwriter in the Boston area. I had finally taken a clerical job to pay the bills, but after less than a month had given that up. I turned to giving piano lessons and within a few weeks had several pupils, their combined fees totaling about sixty dollars per week.

I met Mr. Kevin James in November during one of my pupils' recitals. He'd been dragged along by the child's mother, together with a host of other poor souls, and had stood silently near the back door. As soon as the recital began, he slipped out, and I joined him.

"Enjoying yourself?" I asked.

He leaned languidly against the doorpost. "You go to these affairs often?"

"Naturally. I'm the instructor."

"How do you stand it?"

I shrugged. "Comes with the job. Normally they serve punch later." I tapped the pocket of my well-worn coat. "Punch with a punch."

He grinned. "Don't mind if I do."

We became friends, and he had me to his house for dinner two or three times. One night we'd been speaking of detective stories, and he asked me to join him at the Martha Hudson dinner. I was happy to accept.

The dinner was held at a rambling structure in Arlington Heights known, for some obscure reason, as "The Ranch." The crowd was not exactly what I had expected, consisting mostly of people my own age. They all appeared rather more well-to-do than I, however, which was not surprising.

As drinks were served, we all congregated in the large drawing room, the principal furnishings of which were the bookshelves that lined three of the walls, the huge oil portrait of, I later learned, the Master, and a long table upon which had been set bound copies of some reference works, a violin, a pipe, and a cap. Our host, Mr. Hugo Arrowroot, proposed a toast to Martha Hudson, then to Holmes, after which things assumed a more informal air. We ate a fine dinner of which coq au vin was the main course and, over brandy, fell into a heated discussion concerning the actual existence of fictional characters.

"It all began, I imagine," said Kevin, "with Dante, when he included in his fictional *Divine Comedy* portraits of his enemies. I would suppose it's even an older practice than that."

"Much older," offered another of the guests, a hirsute Harvard student. "All the Greek playwrights did it in their comedies. Aristophanes got in a lot of trouble because of it."

"Not surprising," Kevin continued, "and we're all familiar with historical works that are, finally, more fictitious than the most imaginative novel." Several students chuckled.

Kevin was smoking a briar, sitting on the edge of the table, fingering the open pages of one of the reference works. "But consider this angle. Suppose there was a man whose life was as interesting as could be hoped, and he had a companion who was given to writing. Could that companion refrain from biography? A Boswell to Johnson relationship? I doubt it. But again, suppose that the principal involved eschewed this kind of aggrandizing publicity, for any number of reasons, and forbade his companion to publish. What could they do? One solution would be to publish the biography as a fictional account, using fictional names but actual events.

"I contend that in this theory lies the root of truth in our more celebrated detective heroes." He paused and relit his pipe.

"You're not saying that you think Holmes actually existed?" I said.

"Precisely, John, precisely."

Arrowroot spoke up. "It's not a new theory at all. As far back as 1900, readers were proposing it. Holmes was still alive at that time, remember."

"But a man of his supposed stature?" I protested. "I should think that, even fictionalized, he'd be immediately recognizable to the public."

"James Bond isn't," Kevin said.

"James Bond! Come on."

They shrugged at one another. "It's been established that he's alive and working right now. Of course, though it hurts to admit it, Fleming was better at peripherals than Conan Doyle."

"Peripherals?" I asked.

"You know, names of minor characters, addresses, that sort of thing. Fleming never used real names or addresses, at least so far as we know. And while, of course, Holmes was not named Holmes and didn't live at 221B Baker Street— actually we think he lived in Bond Street near Selfridges— Conan Doyle couldn't help but leave a few characters untouched. He was probably leaving us clues. He had such a fine sense of play. But Hugo, here, is really the expert." He turned to Arrowroot. "Perhaps you'd like to take it from here."

"All right," he said, "but I'm sure we'd all be more comfortable sitting down."

We went out to the hall and brought in more chairs. The novices among us, of whom there were about five including myself, joked about this preposterous theory. When we'd gotten arranged and the brandy had been passed again, Arrowroot, from a large chair near the fireplace, began:

"The characters that Conan Doyle—or should I say Watson?—left intact for us were Martha Hudson and Irene Adler. You're all familiar with Martha Hudson; at least you should be after this evening. She worked for the man who was Holmes until he died in Sussex Downs, after which she came back to London and worked for Lord Peter Thatcher, of the Bank of London, until 1938. She never divulged Holmes's true identity, except of course to Thatcher as a reference. In all probability, Thatcher himself knew long before. In any event, when Thatcher died in the bombings of London, the secret of Holmes's identity was lost forever, since Mrs. Hudson died shortly after she began her retirement, and certainly Conan Doyle never told.

"There was also, as I've said, Irene Adler, 'the only woman,' according to Holmes. She was, indeed, a famous Continental singer in the late 1800s, who disappeared between the years 1892 and 1894. And mark this: those are the very years that Holmes disappeared after following Moriarty to the Reichenbach Falls." He paused for a moment.

"I've read somewhere," ventured another guest, "that letters addressed to 221B Baker Street get answered, though."

Kevin snickered. "Poppycock. A bank clerk answers those letters. They're not even worth considering."

"Kevin's right," Arrowroot continued. "Those 'public' incidentals mean nothing. The man who was Holmes would have never allowed use of so blatant a giveaway. He might just as well have let Conan Doyle use his proper name as his proper address. No, he saw Conan Doyle's clues, and obviously enjoyed them, as he tolerated them. So the path to the truth follows these clues, not the obvious fictions of names and addresses. And there are a few others. Mycroft, for example."

We all looked questioningly at him.

"Mycroft Holmes, Sherlock's brother, the most brilliant man in England. His last name was not Holmes, of course, but we believe his first name was actually Mycroft. He ran the British government single-handedly, especially during World War I. As head of the Secret Service, among other things, he was known as 'M,' a title which I'm sure is familiar to all of you. His initial became the title for the head of British Intelligence. That, by the way, is perhaps Fleming's only slip in the matter of peripherals.

"We also believe that Holmes's code name during World War I was actually Altamont, that he raised bees, injected himself with cocaine, smoked a pipe, and played the violin. What we don't believe is that he actually wrote down a few of his own adventures—that again was Conan Doyle with his sense of play. In all, you see"—he spread his hands out before him—"there is quite a good case."

"But nothing really conclusive," I said.

"Ever the cynic." Kevin smiled. "Well, no, nothing *really*, finally conclusive. No sworn affidavit. But there is one other major bit of evidence that Hugo has overlooked." He looked to Arrowroot. "The articles?"

Our host chuckled. "Oh, yes, of course." He looked at his guests. "If you read the Holmes stories, you will note from time to time that Watson talks of articles—'little monographs,' he calls them—that Holmes has written about any number of subjects, ranging from beekeeping to medicine to musical criticism. Probably the most famous is his treatise on tobaccos and their ashes. All of these articles appeared in periodicals of the times, and all anonymously. So . . . nothing conclusive, but it is an interesting array of facts, isn't it?" He stood up. "I invite you all to look through the reference books I have here, and please, help yourselves to the brandy."

Everyone stood up and gravitated toward the center table. General murmuring once again filled the room. After a few moments, I found myself again with Kevin.

"Very interesting theory," I said.

"You seemed a bit skeptical," he answered lightly, "but it does sound strange on the first hearing, especially if, as you've said, you've never read Conan Doyle."

"Is Holmes really that good?"

He smiled. "He is the Master—of deduction, of disguise, of detection."

I thought for a moment. "Presumably, such a man—a man skilled in the art of detection—would have no trouble escaping detection himself."

"Quite so," Kevin said, "which is why those who have sought to authenticate the Holmes legend have had such a time of it."

I finished my drink and looked at my watch. Quarter past

eleven, and I had students in the morning. I asked Kevin if he were going home by way of Cambridge, and would he mind giving a skeptical friend a lift. We said our good-byes and thanked Arrowroot, then stepped out into the bitter Boston night.

■ ■ ■

I didn't have occasion to think again of that night until nearly five months later.

On January 8, 1983, I received the happy news that four of my songs had been accepted for a television premiere and, with the arrival of a royalty advance, I found myself, at least by my earlier standards, a rich man.

Accordingly, I bid a hasty farewell to my students and to the Boston winter and booked passage on a steamer to Morocco, where I passed the winter and early spring. By mid-April I was anxious to get back to writing, yet in no particular hurry to return to the U.S. One of my songs was having some popular success, and my agent had written several times, asking me to send him a tape as soon as possible. During the three months in Morocco, I had had a fine time but hadn't written a note, so I decided to settle somewhere for the summer and to devote the time to work.

On April 19, I flew from Casablanca to Lyon, France, where a woman I knew had been spending the winter. After looking for several days, we came across an ad in the International Herald Tribune that looked ideal: a summer home, surrounded by oaks and vineyards, with a brook and arbor, near Valence, which is about halfway between Lyon and Marseilles.

I took the train the next day and walked out to the address, a little more than a mile from town. It was an old white adobe house, not too large, and extremely well kept. The owner was a Madame Giraud-Neuilly, a woman nearing seventy whose family, she said, had lived in the house for nearly a century. We spent the afternoon talking and drinking beer. I found her delightful.

Every one of my friends had warned me to beware of the French—that they were a haughty lot, supercilious, and unfriendly. But if Madame Giraud-Neuilly were any example, my friends had been wrong. I spoke French passably well, and that certainly didn't hurt our relationship. At about 5:00, her husband, Jacques Neuilly, came home, and they invited me to stay for dinner. He showed me the wine cellar, which they hadn't used since *le père* had died in the '30s, saying I was welcome to use it for storage if I cared to clean it up. We worked out the details after dinner, and by the time I returned to Lyon the next day, I had a house. Ten days later I moved in.

Since the house was furnished, getting settled took no time at all. I spent the first month working the kinks out of my piano playing and writing daily. I took the five songs with which I'd been happiest, taped them, and sent them to New York; then I decided to take a few days off to celebrate and explore. I started with the cellar, hoping to find some old wine.

The cellar hadn't been used for fifty years, and it looked it. Boxes were lying everywhere, covered with cobwebs. The casks lining the right wall were thick with dust. I turned one of the spigots, and it broke off. I was about to go back upstairs when I noticed something in the far corner reflecting the light from my lantern. I picked my way back and found that I'd been lucky—it was a half case of unopened wine. In the other half of the case lay a sheaf of papers, yellow and brittle, bound by twine. I lifted the whole box and brought it upstairs.

The wine was unlabeled, and I assumed that it was home-made. The sediment was thick on the bottom, and I hadn't been careful enough in moving it. Since I had to let the wine sit for some time before decanting it, I picked up the sheaf of papers, got myself a beer, and went out to the arbor, think-ing only to pass the time until the wine settled.

The papers were written in a thick Continental hand, in French, of course. After I got used to the style, I became en-grossed. I read on, forgetting about the wine, until it got dark, then moved inside and finished the manuscript sitting at the kitchen table. At first I thought it a rather poor at-tempt at a novel, but as I read on, it appeared to be more and more genuine—a personal account of Madame Giraud-Neuilly's father during World War I. But something else was even more interesting to me: if this were a genuine manuscript, it was proof of Arrowroot's theory, for the Auguste Lupa of the manuscript could be none other than Holmes's son.

The next day, I wrote to Madame Giraud-Neuilly, asking her if she could tell me anything about her father's exploits during the war, specifically any undercover operations he might have been involved in. I then set myself to the arduous task of translating.

Within two weeks, I had my landlady's reply. Yes, her fa-ther had been active in the war as some kind of agent. She didn't know too much about it, though, and suggested that I question her half brother, Jean Chessal, who was living in Valence. He was a retired soldier, pushing eighty, and very reluctant to discuss anything with a nosy American. Finally, though, I persuaded him to take the manuscript. A few days later, I went to pick it up.

"Have you read it?" I asked.

"I said I would."

"Well?"

"Well what?"

"What do you think? Is it true?"

He squinted at me through his thick glasses and scratched at his head, as if trying to understand the question.

"How would I know? I wasn't there."

"But your mother . . ."

"My mother was Tania Chessal before she married Jules. What does that prove?"

But of course it proved quite a lot.

I returned home to find a letter from Kevin James. I had written to him asking him to send any information he had regarding Holmes's progeny. The letter was mostly tongue-in-cheek, but it did present several facts about Holmes's relationships, none of which were inconsistent with anything in the manuscript. I'd been slightly bothered by the initials S. H. on Lupa's watch, but Kevin assured me that individuals who used aliases often kept their own initials.

I became angry with myself. After some weeks of translating, I'd become convinced of the manuscript's authenticity, with no more proof than its evident age and its conformance to Hugo Arrowroot's pet theory. There was only one thing to do to finally satisfy myself. Accordingly, I spent most of

the next few months tracking down and interviewing anyone who might have known or worked with the man who
had been Auguste Lupa for the year he lived and worked in
Valence during World War I. Those interviews laid to rest
my every doubt.

■ ■ ■

In translating, I have tried to use contemporary American-
isms wherever possible, though in places where the meaning
is clear from context, I have retained the French.

Finally, I apologize for the prose style in this prologue. I
am not a prose writer by trade, and if I had not come to believe in the importance of this manuscript, I would certainly
have left it where I found it, gathering dust in a wine cellar.

· 1 ·

It was embarrassing, but with a war going on, embarrass-ment was a luxury I couldn't permit myself.

The deep gray and cold of dawn were burning off into a pleasant morning as I walked along the Rue St. Philip in Va-lence, trying to piece together all I'd heard about the man I was to meet and solicit, Auguste Lupa.

We hadn't made an appointment, but I knew where he would be, since every morning he followed a strict routine: up at eight a.m., a walk through the town garden, then a corner table at La Couronne from nine thirty until noon, drinking beer and reading newspapers, nearly always alone. During the afternoons, he would disappear for five hours— no one seemed to know where. He'd then reappear just be-fore six, prepared to work as chef at La Couronne, where he was reputed to be a genius even in this land of chefs *sans pareille*. What was embarrassing was that we needed him, and I was chosen to meet him because of a weakness we shared for beer. We needed him, a chef not yet turned twenty-five, because he was the best spy in Europe.

■ ■ ■

May 18, 1915. The Huns were having a heyday, plumbing the depths to which humanity could sink. They'd already shown their disregard for treaty and commitment by marching across neutral Belgium last August, but the events of this month surprised even those of us who were supposedly inured to their perfidy. Two weeks ago, they'd torpedoed the ship *Lusitania*, killing hundreds of civilians, and on the battlefield at Ypres, they'd just introduced a new element into warfare, the heretofore-outlawed poison gas.

The streets of Valence were filled with red-eyed women whose sons, fathers, and brothers had left for the front, determined to repulse the German invaders.

At ten o'clock this Tuesday morning, I arrived at La Couronne and sat opposite Lupa, whom I'd never before seen. There are some men who can sit in a corner or in a room and simply disappear, blending into their surroundings. If such men make good assassins, this Lupa could never be one. He didn't blend in at all. In fact, he very nearly commanded the entire street, sitting at his table, quietly drinking his beer.

Of course it was he—the high forehead and dark brown hair, combed straight back; the eyes not quite open and yet missing nothing; the heavy lips puckering after every swallow. I, too, had a paper, and settled back to watch him. He was a big man and looked immensely strong, even dressed in an ill-fitting brown suit. His yellow shirt, which would have been garish, or—worse—memorable, on an assassin, was tight across his middle, but didn't bulge at the waist.

The *garçon* came out to his table with two more beers, removed the two empty glasses, and was returning when I stopped him for two of my own. Lupa had set the paper down and was leaning back with a beer. He let the foam settle slightly, then took a deep swallow, draining the contents of the glass in a single gulp. As he lowered the glass to the table, his eyes narrowed slightly, and the corners of his mouth turned suddenly downward.

The *garçon* came with my beer. It was still a bit early, and Lupa and I were the only people there. He looked at me briefly when my beer arrived, and I nodded, the informal recognition of two people sharing the same type of moment. His head inclined a mere centimeter, then turned back to the newspaper.

I reached for the beer and took a small drink, making an elaborate face of disgust. Crossing my legs, I sat back and picked up the paper, stopping every two or three minutes to continue my little charade with the beer: a sip, a look of distaste, meant of course only for myself but obvious to anyone, especially to Lupa. I set the first glass down when I'd finished, and with a little flourish pushed the empty glass as far from me as the table allowed. I then stared down the street, glaring.

Lupa finished his third glass and leaned back with his eyes closed, drumming his fingers methodically on the edge of the table. After a few seconds his fingers came to an abrupt halt, and he glanced over at me.

"*Mal,*" I said with a weak smile.

"*Insupportable!*" He took the other glass and poured it slowly

to the ground. The corners of his mouth turned slightly up-
ward, and he watched me. *"J'en ai marée.* I've had enough."

I took a gamble and decided to make a scene.

"Garçon!"

When he arrived, I spoke too loudly. "This beer is horrible. It is possibly the worst beer in France, and at any rate
it's the worst I've had. This gentleman"—I nodded in Lupa's
direction—"has just poured his to the sidewalk, where it be-
longs, and I only refrain because I deplore waste, especially
during wartime. Take this glass, remove it, and give its contents to the plants or the pigs, then bring me a glass of wine."
I looked at Lupa. "Sir, would you join me in a glass?"

He nodded. "Thank you, I would. And Charles," he said
to the waiter, "don't pour it on the plants or use it in the mus-
tard. Perhaps it wouldn't completely destroy the pork."

He crossed to my table and bowed, more an inclination of
the head than a bow.

"Auguste Lupa," he said.

"Jules Giraud." I motioned to the empty chair.

We sat, and he began to talk.

"I, too, sir, deplore waste, though I could argue that there
was no waste involved in pouring that beer to the ground.
That beer was waste when it arrived, and what pains me is
that I've been putting up with it for months now. I am in-
debted to you, Monsieur Giraud. Sometimes I need a nudge
to act, though I generally decide instantly on matters of
taste; but I have an inordinate fondness for beer, and since
good beer cannot be purchased here, I've allowed my integrity an unforgivable laxity." He closed his eyes and sighed,

and there was, indeed, a burden of sadness around him. "It will be hard without beer, but my taste applauds yours, sir."

The wine arrived, and he raised his glass, after first sniffing it and looking through the dark red liquid. *"Santé,"* he said, "and damn this war."

We both drained our glasses. He signaled for another, and I began to smile.

"You're amused?" he asked.

"It seems strange," I said, raising the second glass, "to find myself agreeing with a man whose major concern in the midst of European destruction is the lack of quality beer."

"But you do agree."

"Of course, damn it." I smiled again. "The living must continue to live. But you are wrong about something," I said.

"And that is . . . ?"

"The dearth of good beer. There is a great quantity of excellent beer not four kilometers from where we sit. But it is not for sale."

He looked at me patiently and warily. "Monsieur Giraud, I don't know you, but you don't seem given to idle jesting. I have been cooking here in Valence for the winter and have searched tirelessly for a supply of good beer, and to no avail. I have some talent at discovering things that people try to keep hidden, and there is no beer."

"There is, and it is hidden, and privately brewed by a man who values his privacy. No more than six men know of it."

"They are very discreet men," he said.

"Very," I continued. "They have to be, but that's no matter. Even knowing that the beer exists, you would never find it, for you're not likely to see me again and you don't know the other five." I drained my glass and got up to go. "It's been a pleasant morning, sir," I said. "Good luck."

I hadn't gone ten paces when he spoke.

"Monsieur Giraud."

I turned. "Yes?"

"Would your chef mind terribly if you missed a meal?"

"He goes nearly mad," I said, "but occasionally—" I stopped abruptly. "How did you know I had a chef?"

He nodded, his eyes narrowing somewhat, perhaps with humor. "You've just confirmed it."

"Yes, but . . ."

"Monsieur Giraud," he said. "There was nothing sinister, I assure you, in the question. It was mere conjecture."

"But how . . . ?"

"Simplicity itself. It's clear that you are a man of taste regarding your palate. Your clothing further bespeaks a certain degree of wealth, and your accent—indeed, even the way you hold a wineglass—betrays good breeding. Finally, your coloring is pale."

"Yes?"

"Surely that is enough."

I laughed in spite of myself. "I'm afraid I don't follow you."

He ticked off the steps of his deduction with the fingers of his right hand. "First, you can afford a chef. Second, you would demand fine meals, especially at home. Third, if you yourself spent the required amount of time behind a hot stove, your complexion would be ruddy like my own. It is not. Ergo, you have a chef."

"You're very astute," I said.

He waved it off. "It's nothing. Child's play. Literally, in my case. My father was something of a stickler for such matters. I've kept it up as a hobby, more or less. Just now I made an educated guess, and your reaction confirmed it. True deduction is a closed system—it confirms itself."

"Still, I'm impressed."

"Well, then perhaps you'll permit me to impress you with my small skills as a chef. Would you care to lunch?" The eyes were sharp now, though the face was relaxed and friendly.

"It's rather early," I said, hesitating a moment.

He continued. "Egg of pigeon poached in red wine, escargots, *rognons aux fines herbes,* all accompanied by the finest wine on the Côte du Rhone, served at the chef's table."

"It is a great temptation," I said. "You, of course, though you haven't said it, would greatly appreciate an introduction to a certain local brewer I mentioned."

He smiled. "Your deduction, though obvious, is flawless."

"And your discretion?"

"Unimpeachable."

I walked back to him.

"At what time shall we eat?" I asked. Later I would recognize that slight turn of the lips as a beaming smile.

"We can begin immediately, if you'd like to come down to the kitchen."

"Gladly."

We crossed through the tables to a door that didn't leave much room to spare for us and opened it. A short stairway led to the kitchen. He stopped at the bottom.

"And the introduction?"

"Pardon?"

"To the brewer?"

"Ah yes. You've already met him."

He raised his eyebrows. "Indeed?"

I nodded. *"A vôtre service."*

And so it was arranged that Auguste Lupa come to my house the next morning at ten for beer and a light lunch.

· 2 ·

Espionage, like any other profession, has its ups and downs. Lately, though, it had taken a monotonous turn to the latter.

I'd been one of the few operatives who'd dared before August to suggest that the German thrust would be through Belgium. This was viewed as so outrageous that those of us who believed it were "transferred." Even after the event came to pass, we were still regarded as second-class and relegated to desks or to the country. I should have been upset with the demotion, but in fact I'd been happy. I'd begun to feel constrained under the inflexibility of Joffre's* yoke.

Consequently, I had spent the past autumn behind a desk, doing nothing worthwhile, and had finally, much to my relief, been called back to my hometown for this case. It was to be a break in my routine, a kind of forced vacation. No

*Commander in chief of French army.

sooner had I returned to the little white house, nestled snugly amid grapevines and a small grove of oaks, however, than my contact had suddenly been taken dead—officially, an accidental drowning.

The next month I'd busied myself with the beer and light gardening, spending much time with my new chef, a young Swiss with extraordinary promise named Fritz Benet. It had been a pleasant enough time, or would have been without the specter of murder hanging over the house. Normally, living in an atmosphere where people tend to die unexpectedly didn't overly disturb my peace of mind, but somehow, at home, I found it quite annoying.

There were, of course, my friends. Marcel Routier, my closest friend and fellow agent (though we rarely worked together) was now in Valence. My other friends, to whom we were traveling salesmen, included Henri Pulis, a Greek shop owner in town; Paul Anser, an American poet of some small repute; and Georges Lavoie, an Alsatian salesman who dealt in hospital supplies. Including Fritz, then, these were the other five men who knew about the beer.

There was also Tania. I had told Lupa that only five other men in town knew about the beer, and Tania—tall and slim, with long black hair and deep, deep eyes and voice—was as far from being a man as any creature on earth.

Marcel had been sent down after my original contact had "drowned" and had told me the problem. It was believed that the man behind most of the assassinations in the past two years—including Francis Ferdinand's in Sarajevo—was now living and working out of Valence. How intelligence had come to believe that, I had no idea, since there wasn't a shred of evidence that pointed to the involvement of a mastermind assassin. Yes, last spring an agent in Valence had been found with a bullet in his head two days after wiring that he was onto something big. But "something big" could mean just about anything these days, what with half the nations of Europe at war.

There was, in fact, only one event of importance, of real significance, attached to this locale, and that was the arrival, early the previous fall, of Auguste Lupa.

Obviously, that wasn't his real name, but no one had any idea of what it really was, so it didn't matter. In Belgrade, he'd been Julius Adler. At Sarajevo, he was Cesar Mycroft. In Milan . . . but the list is immaterial, though impressive. Always a reference to one of the Caesars in one of the names—perhaps some family connection. We'd followed him when he broke out of jail in Belgrade a year ago June, lost him briefly, found him again in Geneva, trailing him to Valence. When he actually took a job here, I'd been sent.

Lupa was the unparalleled genius among the agents of Europe and he seemed to work for himself, for no government acknowledged him. As far as we knew, he'd been approached before, by us as well as the British and Russians, and to all he'd feigned an absolute innocence of any knowledge of espionage or even of the affairs of politics. His loves, he said, included only food and beer. In spite of his protestations of naivete, he'd been jailed for espionage in three countries and had turned over quantities of information, always by leaving a bag loaded with papers in a locker somewhere. The material was always typed, never on the same machine, never with the same paper, almost never in the same language, and always frighteningly exact. He was the best, and he'd been trying to discover the brains behind Europe's assassinations for two years. He obviously wanted us here, or he wouldn't have let himself be followed, and yet he'd made no overtures of any sort and had forced me to contact him. It was barely possible that he didn't suspect my associations, but it was probable that even as I sat down across from him, he was cataloguing everything he knew about me, deciding the time was right, and letting me set the tone of our relationship.

During lunch, I had asked him if he'd mind if a friend of mine were present at the next day's meeting, and he'd said no. Accordingly, I invited Marcel Routier, and he arrived early the next morning, a little past nine o'clock. We sat outside in the sun for our coffee.

"He, of course, knows us," he said.

I shrugged. "It's nearly certain, but he may have been so attuned to his own inquiries that they haven't crossed ours yet. In any case, we'll see before long."

He sipped at his coffee, took a bite of Fritz's blueberry muffin, and looked out over the grounds. His hair was the color of straw, which made it look as though there was less of it than there was. It was a bit too long for my taste, just touching the tops of his ears, which he said was to make up for the lack on top. This morning he was wearing white pants and shoes, and a high-collared blue shirt, and, except possibly for his face, he looked much more the dandy than the spy. A lot of women had found him attractive, but I couldn't understand why. Tania had said he had classic features, but too many of them. His forehead and nose commanded his face except when he smiled, at which time his teeth commanded everything. He was smiling now.

"Damn," he said, "I wish I'd thought of getting Lupa with beer. Occasionally you show real genius, Jules."

"Perception and devotion, hardly genius. When Fritz told me of the food at La Couronne, it started me thinking. A man who could cook as well as he did, who smuggled in spices for the integrity of his dishes, and yet who spent every morning drinking swill on the sidewalk . . . no, it didn't make sense. That man's taste buds were too refined for that beer, but he loves beer. Simple, actually."

"Like Columbus's egg," he said.

■   ■   ■

At first, even at Lupa's insistence, Fritz would not come to the table with us, but finally he overcame his prejudice against the chef dining with his patron when Lupa got him engrossed in a recipe for pheasant.

"The problem," he said, "is that too often that delicate bird is overwhelmed by tarragon and sage, when it should be coaxed into accepting their favors, as a woman might accept other favors, with a little wine. Set the spices in the wine first, several hours before, and leave it chilled. Then—"

"Gentlemen," I said, "I don't mean to interrupt, but couldn't we continue this discussion at the table?"

So the four of us sat to savor Fritz's delicious sole and honey, followed by a subtle tournedos Béarnaise. The two chefs were very close to the same age, and they seemed to get along exceptionally well, which made the lunch even smoother than it would have been with the fine food. There was no hint of recognition between them when I introduced

Marcel and Lupa, though once during the meal they glanced at one another after a remark Fritz had made about the state of cuisine in the Balkans.

"And now," I said, as we were finishing our coffee, "shall we go to the cellar? Fritz, will you prepare the arbor?"

"He is a sensitive chef," Lupa said when Fritz had gone. "Has he been with you long?"

"Actually, no. Less than a year."

"Do you know where he was trained?"

A look of annoyance crossed Marcel's countenance. Lupa must have seen it too, for he held up his hand and continued quickly. "I only ask about his training because it is so evidently superlative. The man is nearly a *maître*, and at his age that is very rare, indicative of great native skill and rigorous apprenticeship. As a chef myself, I would be interested to know where he studied."

"To tell you the truth, I'm not at all certain. He arrived here on the recommendation of a mutual friend, and his cooking has never given me cause to question his background. My friend was living in Strasbourg before the hostilities began, so I gather he trained in one of the establishments there."

"In Germany, then?"

Finally Marcel got in a word. "That point is most arguable, isn't it?"

"Strasbourg is a German city," Lupa asserted.

"Strasbourg is French! It will always be French, regardless of who its rulers might be."

"Gentlemen, please!" I felt I had to step in or tempers, specifically Marcel's, would flare.

For an instant Lupa seemed inclined to glare and continue the debate, but as I watched him, he swiftly conquered his rising emotions. He spoke contritely. "You're right, of course, Monsieur Routier. I apologize. Strasbourg must once again fly the tricolor. I only meant to comment favorably upon Fritz's cuisine, and I'm afraid my youth carried me into irrelevancies. He is a fine, fine chef—and you, Monsieur Giraud, are a lucky man to have him."

There was an awkward moment as Marcel brought himself back under control, but I could see that Lupa's obvious sincerity had made its mark.

"Well," I said, clapping my hands, "should we begin the tour?"

We all rose from the table and I led the two down to my cellar, the left half of which was reserved for wines and the other for the beer apparatus. There were five stone crocks lined against the right wall, and the smell of yeast and ripening beer lent an aroma that I found pleasant to the room, but I knew it might prove too strong to a novice, even a beer-loving novice.

"As long as the wine isn't opened down here," I said, explaining, "it is ideal."

As we walked along, I went over some of the steps in the brewing, and seeing the two of them smile patiently, I suggested we proceed to the tasting.

Off to the side of the house, I was blessed with a small arbor of trees, through which ran a clear stream where Fritz stored butter and beer. It was perfectly chilled, and I'd built a table of thick oak, where my friends and I came to sit and relax, out of the glare. We walked out to that table now and silently sat while Fritz brought the beer, left the bottles with us, and departed.

Lupa drank his whole glass at one swill, just as he had the day before at La Couronne, and yet conveyed the impression that he was savoring every drop. Marcel and I drank more slowly but with no less enjoyment. Lupa put down his glass and looked at me.

"Remarkable."

"It pleases you?"

"There are certain advantages to being raised a rich man, eh?" said Marcel. "Certain opportunities to develop talents which otherwise would be buried under the mundane cares of survival." He looked at Lupa, smiling. "He constantly makes me envious. Such beer, such a house, such a chef . . ."

"Such beer," Lupa repeated, leaning back with his eyes closed.

I poured him another glass. For the next quarter of an hour we sat quietly enjoying the day, the beer, and . . . was it the company or the suspense? It seemed to me that we were all waiting for another to be the first to speak. Finally, I ventured cautiously, "Monsieur Lupa, what brings you here to Valence? Could you not accomplish your goals elsewhere, in a larger city?"

He looked at me quizzically, the touch of a smile lifting the corners of his mouth.

"What goals are those?" he asked.

"Oh, the usual for a young chef. Apprenticeship in a large hotel, assistantship to a master—"

But he cut me off. "A man who follows the usual routes obtains the usual results. Like so many other endeavors, cuisine is both an art and a skill. Of course, the French scoff at such an idea—meaning no offense to you, sir. Too often the path to excellence at a skill is a limiting experience, until the mind, finally, is trained to abhor innovation. And, beyond a certain mastery of skills, innovation is what lets a chef stand alone."

When he finished his little speech, he had none of the habits one would expect from one so young, neither the slight embarrassment nor the brash defiance that often punctuates the speech of the insecure. Rather, he reached for his beer and drank.

"It's clear," said Marcel, "that you wish to stand alone."

"Only a dullard would not."

There was a moment of uncomfortable silence.

Finally, Marcel spoke. "But surely you don't mean that."

Lupa nodded. "If I hadn't meant it, I wouldn't have said it."

"What of our men at the front, then? They don't stand alone. In fact, all our hope resides in their fighting together, in the assumption that there are goals that must take precedence over individuality. Are all our soldiers dullards?"

"Probably most. It's always rather meaningless to generalize. Joffre certainly is."

"Then you wouldn't fight?" Marcel was getting angry.

Lupa took a breath. "Fortunately, I'm a citizen of the United States, and we are presently neutral. I'm afforded the luxury of not fighting."

"But would you?"

"I wouldn't like to be mere cannon fodder."

"Because you wish to stand alone."

"Exactly." He drank some beer. "But I see you're getting

upset with me. I don't mean to say that I don't believe in causes, or that everyone should have individuality. I applaud our troops at the front. I only refer to men of adequate intelligence, and they are not so commonplace as is generally believed, who attain eminence in a field and then prove themselves incompetent because they lack imagination, individuality, call it what you will. Joffre can execute all the textbook moves. What he cannot do is adapt. Luckily for France, the Germans are even more stupid, or they would have taken Paris months ago." He paused and drank again.

"The key then . . ." said Marcel.

"Is innovation," Lupa continued. "I don't mean to slur those who follow others' examples, or those who learn a trade and become proficient at a skill. No. We need them. I simply bemoan the lack of creative leadership by people who are, nominally, our leaders."

"I quite agree," I put in.

"Perhaps I misunderstood," said Marcel. "Then you are here as a head chef to learn to innovate?"

Lupa smiled. "One doesn't learn how to innovate. One simply acts, and learns from his actions. But yes, I am here to become a chef. I am already a cook."

It seemed that Marcel was on the verge of questioning him directly about his real work. He leaned toward the younger man with a gleam in his eyes. A slight breeze came into the arbor, though, and Lupa, rubbing his hands together, stood.

"Gentlemen," he said, "I have very much enjoyed the day, but I must now attend to other matters. I'm becoming more and more a creature of habit, and my habits won't brook much flexibility. I'm afraid I must go."

"Well, if you must, you must," I said, "but would you consider coming back this evening? Once a week, I host a gathering of the men I had earlier mentioned to you, and I'm always happy to find another discerning beer lover."

He bowed slightly. "I'd be delighted, though it would have to be after the dinner hour."

"Around ten, then."

We remained seated and watched him until he entered the house. He walked very lightly for a man of his size.

"Well?" asked my friend.

I shrugged. "What do you think of him?"

"He's very polite."

We laughed, and I rose to get some more beer. When I had come back and sat down, Marcel was still smiling.

"He doesn't seem to be in as much a hurry to enlist our aid as we are to enlist his, does he?"

"Hardly. And I must admit that after all this time, I'm starting to wonder if I've been put out to pasture, that there's nothing happening in Valence, and I've been sent here to sit out the war with my cook and my beer. Have you heard of anything at all?"

"I heard from Paris late last week; it must have been after last Wednesday's gathering, and they told us to sit tight, that whatever would happen here obviously was in the planning stage, and the longer the wait, the greater the odds that it's really something big." He took a long drink of beer. "The damn thing is, there's no one worth assassinating here, and no

one scheduled to come, and not a clue of planning in progress . . ." He trailed off. "Nothing."

"Is it possible," I asked, "that this time it won't be an
assassination? Suppose, for example, it's sabotage, or kidnap-
ping, or . . ."

"No, I doubt it," he said. "Our man directs killers, and if
we could just think of . . . my God!" He'd put down the
glass and was staring so intently into the trees behind us that
I turned around.

"What is it?"

"He is here to assassinate."

"Impossible," I said. "There's not a man in this region of
any strategic importance, and no one will be . . ."

"There's one," he said, his eyes shining.

"Who's that?"

"Auguste Lupa."

We sat for a moment or two in silence, while I thought of
objections to what he'd said. In the first place, Lupa had arrived on the trail of our man, but that of course could be a
way to have Lupa where he wanted him. Come to Valence
so that Lupa would come here, so that he could kill him
here? That was far-fetched, and I said so. Why Valence?

"Possibly because Lupa has an embarrassing connection
here, and killing him in sordid surroundings would not only
be good propaganda but would rid Germany of the agent they
most feared." Marcel was warming now to his own suggestion.

"But there would be no propaganda, since the public has
never heard of Lupa, since Lupa wasn't even his name a few
months ago. Finally, Marcel, he would never have waited so
long to move. If he had known who Lupa was and where he

would find him, he would have acted and cleared out months ago."

"You're probably right," he conceded, "but he's here for something, and we don't have any idea of who he is, what he wants, or why he's here. We must ask Lupa what he has on him, and tonight."

"It will be difficult at the gathering," I said.

"Then later."

"We'll see, but I can't shake the feeling that the man is here for sabotage."

"To sabotage what? There's nothing here in Valence."

"No, not in Valence itself. But there is the arms factory in St. Etienne, surely close enough to warrant investigation. You know as well as I that all our major defense research is going on there. Our man would also know. Otherwise, why would Lupa be here? It's got to be something damned important. If that factory is blown . . . well, it'll set us back over a year."

He looked down at the ground and picked up his beer. "It's guarded, of course."

"It's impregnable."

"Well, there you are."

"No. What bothers me is its seeming invulnerability. There are enough troops guarding the place, all right, but in a sense that is really not the point. It can't be directly assaulted, which is of course why they'd have to send a man here—to break it, to find a way in."

"How is security?"

"I tell you, Marcel, that's what puzzles me so much about it. Everything is as it should be. It is completely impossible.

It can't be entered by anyone who hasn't been thoroughly checked out. Everyone who works inside has been cleared and cleared again. There are troops all over St. Etienne with 75s ready to shoot down any aeroplanes . . ."

"Aeroplanes?"

"Probably not, I agree, but one can't be too careful."

"Well, then, it seems as if it's all covered."

"It is, and that's what bothers me. The level of security may have created a degree of complacency. I'm growing more and more certain that we should direct our attentions there. It would also explain why our man has stayed around so long without acting. He couldn't very well break their security in too short a time."

"If at all."

I looked across at my friend. Years of service still hadn't forced him to develop an imagination. He was steady and loyal, always ready for action, and totally without fear, but he could never foresee an event before its occurrence. The times I had worked with him before, he'd been invaluable, but as an active force, rather more like another weapon. And so I'd developed a protective attitude toward him. Not that he needed protection from any known danger—once it was identified, he was in his element. Too often, however, he suspected nothing and would have walked into traps totally unprepared. I don't know how he was with other agents. Perhaps we had been friends for so long that he didn't feel with me that he had to be so much the professional, that our personal relations overlapped. I didn't share his feeling, but he was my closest friend. Now, as I discussed possibilities with him, I couldn't get rid of the feeling that perhaps it was approaching the time for him to get out of espionage. He would perhaps be more valuable as a strategist, directing troops from a defensible position against a visible enemy.

"Time will tell," I answered him.

"Yes."

We got up and started to cross over to the house. A breeze was blowing steadily now, and it felt as if rain was in the air. I put my arm around my friend's shoulder.

"Let's find something," I said. "I'm getting very bored."

He laughed. "Better to be bored than dead. There's a lot of that going around these days."

"Yes," I said, keeping my thoughts to myself. Overhead, the sky had begun to darken.

· 3 ·

It had rained before the first of the guests arrived, and now the clouds hung low over the land, spent and yet threatening. Occasionally there was a low roar of thunder—the first thunderstorm of the season—but the clouds obscured the lightning.

Georges Lavoie and Henri Pulis arrived first, a little after eight o'clock, and we sat by the front window looking out over the field that lay between my home and the road, some seventy-five meters away. Through some fluke the oaks that surrounded the house did not mar the view out of this window, though with the wind and the swirling branches the scene was neatly translated from the pastoral to the Gothic. From time to time one of the lower branches would sweep across the window like a hand. Twice the wind was strong enough to throw a hail of acorns into the glass, sounding for all the world like the tapping knuckles of that passing hand.

It was, I suppose, a rather strange collection of guests that came every week to my house and shared my beer. We were not confreres by occupation or age; indeed, we had almost nothing in common except a love of beer and companionship. I was by far the eldest, except for Marcel, and the only one of us with any wealth. Usually, we would drink and talk, often playing cards, until midnight. Sometimes Paul Anser would read something he'd just written, horribly translated. He was a great joker and kept the nights far from being dull. Now, with the war, we never ran out of news to discuss, though some nights we still would just sit and read, as in an English men's club, with of course the notable exception of Tania.

Henri Pulis looked like what he was—one of the hardworking bourgeoisie. Though he was some fifteen years younger than I, his hair was nevertheless starting to streak with gray, and his face was set in creases punctuated by a large, drooping black mustache. He always sat slumped over, and this made him look even shorter than he was. Now he sat, nervously yet methodically wiping the foam from his mustache with his left hand, holding the beer in his right.

He'd come to Valence as a young man, perhaps ten years ago, after working for a time as a ship's mate. It was even rumored that he'd deserted from the Greek navy when his ship had docked at Marseilles, and he had moved north, lying low for some months until he decided it was safe to appear. After two or three years, he'd saved enough to open his own shop. We had met because he sold the supplies I needed for the beer, and though he was not as witty as the others, he was no less popular. He often seemed uncomfortable until he'd had a few beers; then he would relax and entertain us with crude jokes that we were all secretly ashamed of enjoying. He had originally come when I'd asked him, he said, to get away from his wife and six children, and though by now we were all friends, I was still not completely convinced that he so much treasured our company as that he considered it a respite from his family's.

Georges Lavoie normally came with Henri. They were friends who often dined together during the weeks when both were free. Georges was thirty-five or thereabouts, a traveling salesman who was often on the road but who made a point of returning by Wednesday, when we all gathered. He was kept from the service by a severe limp—his right leg was shorter than his left. But this didn't hamper him from somehow seeming the most urbane member of our fellowship. His father had been a banker in Brussels, in Lille, even in Coblentz, before he finally settled in Metz, and undoubtedly the company of bankers had instilled in him a certain conservatism of dress and deference in mannerism. Nevertheless, he had a ready tongue and a stock of stories which were the more amusing for their incongruity. He, along with Tania and myself, never drank to excess, while the other three often left the house a bit affected. When the war broke out, he had left his native Alsace-Lorraine and fled south. He worked now out of Valence, selling and delivering his wares to factories, hospitals, and arsenals in the towns along the Rhone. He was the latest of our number, except for Lupa.

Henri shuddered, crossing one leg over the other and reaching for his bottle. "Good night to get drunk," he said.

"It's a good night for something," Georges agreed philo-
sophically.

I raised my glass. "To something," I said, and we drank
the toast.

Fritz brought in three more beers and left the room, shaking his head sadly. He did not like beer at all.

By now it had gotten dark. The lamps were lit, and the
fire stoked, and we had moved to more comfortable seats.
We always remained in the big sitting room for these evenings.
With its large front window reflecting the lights back in on
us, the warm rug, and the variety of furniture, it was ideal
for a small gathering of friends. Last spring, before I was sent
north, we'd met in the arbor several times, but somehow, after dark, this room was much more comfortable.

Georges and Henri sat on either side of the large fireplace, which commanded one corner of the room, next to
the entrance to the dining area and, behind that, the kitchen.
I sat on the divan under the window, looking out for the
others' arrival. In the far corner, away from me, were two
other stuffed chairs, with a coffee table in front, then the
door leading in from the foyer. Just to my left was a china
closet and, to my right, bookshelves that lined the wall from
the corner to the fireplace. Two other tables held our beer
and some magazines, one directly in front of me, the other
between Henri and Georges.

The house was really too large for me, but this room was
ideal. For a time I'd busied myself with improvements, moving the water closet indoors, installing a shower; but then I'd
given up and left the other rooms vacant until Fritz had

moved in the year before. I slept in the one upstairs room, directly overhead.

From outside came the sound of a carriage drawing up, and laughter, and in a moment Marcel entered with Paul and Tania.

"Don't bother getting up," said Paul. "Just bring a beer for the hero. Fritz!" he yelled. "Fritz!"

Tania crossed over to me and kissed me after she'd sat down. "He really was terrific! The horse bolted and was starting to run as we met Paul down the road, and he jumped on its back like a red Indian and calmed it."

"It was nothing—really, I assure you—that any American couldn't do. Riding on the plains for days at a time with only stale bread and . . ."

Marcel was laughing. "Sure, Paul, sure. Fritz, bring him his beer before he tells us about fighting the Indians."

The beer arrived and the newcomers drank.

Paul Anser stood grinning in the middle of the room. He wore his "flyer's jacket," as he called it, a leather affair with a woolen collar; heavy boots; pants that looked to be made out of canvas.

"What a night," he said, "and hello everyone. Your beer is getting no worse, Jules. Are we late? Is there time to catch up with Henri?"

Henri smiled. "Only my second," he lied.

"Ah. Fritz—how are you, Fritz?—two more beers, please. Mustn't let Henri get the jump on me."

Marcel took Paul's jacket, and they both sat—Marcel on the divan with Tania and me, and Paul next to the entrance to the kitchen.

"There must be something in the air," I said. "Henri just said it was a fine night to get drunk."

"Well, by God, let's get to it." Paul poured his second beer.

"Hear, hear," said Tania, surprisingly, "and then Paul can read for us."

"Alcohol can't hurt my accent. When I slur I sound more French."

"Hardly more French," said Georges, "possibly less American." And we all laughed.

I leaned back with my arm around Tania and listened to the banter, trying to find a good moment to tell them we would have a new guest. We were so relaxed now together that I almost regretted having invited Lupa, but I'd had the same doubts about Georges, and they'd proven groundless. I was finding it difficult to divorce business from my day-to-day life when living at home. The people I met socially had always been friends, and though I liked Lupa, my motive for inviting him was certainly not friendship.

Tania sat easily next to me, sipping her beer and joining in with the others. Twenty-one years ago she'd married Jean Chessal, one of my neighbors, and over the years had borne him four children, all boys. Jean had been in the service his entire life, and it was natural for the boys to follow him, especially with the war looming. Her husband had been killed in the first weeks of the war, and now the boys were at the front, all miraculously unhurt—so far. She was brave, cheerful without any visible effort, witty, and very beautiful. We had been lovers, now, for six years.

She was not a native of Valence, or even of this region, and even after so many years, her accent betrayed a certain foreignness which I found becoming. When Chessal had returned to Valence with his new bride, there had been rumors of royal ancestry, of some distinctly romantic past. I had no trouble accepting her with this touch of mystery. When we first met, I had been fascinated, but now her antecedents meant no more to me than her accent.

The others had gone on for a time with Paul and finally persuaded him to begin reading a new poem. He wanted more beer, but I'd given Fritz a sign to hold off until everyone had arrived.

After token comments relating to the paucity of his host's refreshments, Paul went to the center of the room and began. He read in English, which only two or three of us understood, and it was quite modern, but he read well—the cadences were rhythmic and pleasing. This was, after all, his only live audience of any size.

When he'd finished, I told him I found the thing incomprehensible, but he didn't seem to mind. He just shrugged and grinned and said something about comic relief, though while he was reading, he did not seem to take it lightly. Suddenly, he turned and cried out:

"I must, must, simply must have more beer!"

Henri, who had sat looking utterly perplexed while Paul read, concurred with a shy belch.

Georges stood and raised his empty glass. "I'd propose a toast to the poet if there were something to drink."

Tania turned to me. "Why are you holding the beer, Jules? Is there some surprise for us?"

The damned woman knew me too well.

"What makes you think I'm holding back the beer?" I asked.

Paul spoke. "You'll never understand women, Jules. Our most secret thoughts are the common currency of their lives. Maybe they don't read the thought but they sense the secret; and although maybe they know less, they understand more."

"Bah!" Georges interjected. "I may be only a simple observer, but I know when a gaffe has been committed. For a man to pretend to understand women is bad manners."

"And for him to really understand them is bad morals," Tania added.

"All right. *Assez, assez*. I've been holding back the beer. I admit it. I'm guilty, but there's a reason."

"One would hope so," said Tania.

"Such a serious matter," added Georges.

"It's not such a great matter," I said, smiling. "We're going to have another guest." I looked around for reactions, but there was nothing special. Henri looked a bit put out for a moment, but I had expected that. As one who cherished his nonintellectuality and tried as much as possible to keep the conversation off-color, he was not disposed to welcome a new guest who might tip the balance of the evening away from purely sensual enjoyment.

"Who is this person, Jules?" Georges asked. "We know almost everyone in Valence. Is he a neighbor?"

"Jules hasn't said our guest is a he, Georges. Perhaps he has invited another woman." Marcel looked at Tania and winked.

"Enough." It was time to end the mystery. "Our guest is Auguste Lupa. I met him quite casually the other day at

La Couronne. He is a connoisseur of good beer, and a very pleasant fellow. Nothing more. He's arrived here only recently, and I thought he would enjoy a taste—shall I say of society? I think he'll fit in very nicely with our group." The door sounded. "Ah, that would be him."

Fritz brought Lupa into the room and announced him grandly.

The big man stood for a moment framed in the doorway, looking at the assemblage. There was a moment of silence, and then I jumped up and performed the introductions. Only Henri seemed ill at ease, while the others nodded cautiously and Fritz went to get another round of beers. Lupa sat by the door and, after another moment, spoke.

"Please disregard my attendance here for a time. Since you are obviously all attuned to one another, you'll want to continue as before. Don't make allowances for me. After a time the novelty will be gone, and I'll join in as one of you, but for now, let me drink quietly and not disturb you."

It was a strange prologue and served more to reinforce the silence than to dispel it.

"Nonsense," said I. "Why don't you tell the group about yourself? It isn't every day we welcome a new member."

"Member?"

"Well, not really a member of anything. Sometimes we do refer to ourselves as a group of sorts, but nothing so rigid as to demand membership."

"Do tell us about yourself," said Tania.

I saw Marcel smile at me. I didn't expect Lupa to drop any information, but having him talk for a while wouldn't hurt.

"Yeah, like where are you from?" That was Paul.

Lupa looked at him. "You're American," he said, then
continued almost as though talking to himself. "Northwest,
I should say. No, not so far west, perhaps Wyoming or
Montana."

"You got it, mister. Missoula, Montana, U. S. of A. How
'bout you?"

"Born."

"Pardon?"

"Born in America, not bred. My mother traveled quite a
lot with her career and fortuitously timed my birth so that I
became an American citizen at the time of my first breath."

"You don't talk like an American," said Henri, "more like
a Greek, or . . ."

"Or a Serbian?" ventured Georges.

Lupa smiled. "Exactly. I've never lived in America,
though I would like to go there. I was raised by several of my
relatives—in England primarily but in other parts of Europe
as well."

I was surprised to find him so conversational. He sat
straight in his chair, genial and relaxed. Henri and Marcel
took out their pipes and lit them, Henri with a bit of ember
from the fire.

Lupa raised his head slightly and sniffed at the air. "Ah,
the smell of pipes. I love them. They bring back memory of
my childhood, of my father. You, Monsieur Routier, you're
having a Cavendish latakia mixture, are you not? And Monsieur Pulis—a Virginia tobacco, perhaps even a chewing plug
if I'm not mistaken?"

The two men looked at each other, impressed. "Exactly,"
Marcel said.

"Not to chew, but to smoke," Henri said, his face showing a certain sullenness.

I interjected. "You know your tobaccos, monsieur."

He nodded. "It was a special interest of my father. Once we were together in Paris, and . . ."

"Oh, then you're not new to France?" asked Tania, interrupting. "I'd somehow thought you were."

"No, I spent most of my summers here as a youth." He stopped and looked at Tania and me. "I should say when I was more of a youth."

"What do you do in Valence?" Henri asked suddenly and, I thought, rather belligerently.

Lupa looked carefully at him. "You bear me animus, sir?"

I stepped in. "You'll have to excuse Monsieur Pulis. He isn't happy about having a new member, no matter who it might be. I'm sure it's nothing personal. Isn't that right, Henri?"

"If you'd prefer that I leave . . ."

"No, no, don't be silly. It's I who should leave," said Henri. "I'm sorry. Sometimes I forget myself. I act like the ass."

"Sometimes we all do," Lupa replied with a pleasant smile. "Such is the effect that troubles sometimes have on us."

Henri nodded, taking another huge drink from his bottle. Then, in a kind of double take, he put down his glass and stared at Lupa.

Georges, however, was the first to speak. "What do you know of Henri's troubles?" The others all nodded in shared suspicion.

Lupa, aware of his faux pas, was nearly successful in smiling. Then he spoke in a self-deprecating tone. "You mustn't mind me, please. Sometimes I get carried away by assumptions I can't help making, and they lead me to conclusions that are often ridiculous. I saw Monsieur Pulis sitting slightly slumped over, and the thought entered my head that he seemed unnaturally subdued, given the spirit of the occasion. Additionally, I noticed that the second button on his shirt is missing and that he wears a wedding ring. He is, therefore, married, but on bad terms with his wife just now, or she wouldn't have let him go out with his shirt unmended. Finally, he appears to be drinking much more than the rest of us, often a sign of someone trying to forget a particularly depressing or difficult situation."

Henri's hand had gone to the missing button. His face clouded over; then he grinned sheepishly. "I've got to be more careful," he said, somewhat enigmatically.

I had earlier marveled at Lupa's perspicacity, so I was prepared to some extent for his displays. The others, I noticed, were beginning to look as though they felt slightly apprehensive, as though they were all unwittingly under some unseen magnifying glass. Before anyone else could comment, however, Fritz entered with the beer, walked to the various seats, and deposited the new bottles, setting a glass before Lupa. He might have simply brought the tray into the room, but the pride he took in his work demanded that certain rituals be performed.

We looked to Tania, who by tradition delivered the first toast after the whole company had assembled. We had not all opened the bottles yet, which Fritz refused to do because, he said, of the danger. Once a bottle had exploded as he was about to open it, a common enough occurrence with home-brewed beer, and since then he'd refused to participate in any opening.

Tania looked at Lupa and then at the rest of us. Georges was still fiddling with his bottle, but she began.

"To our new guest, M. Lupa, and . . ."

Before she could say, "and to France," there was a loud pop, and Georges was grabbing his right hand with his left, swearing. We all leapt up and crossed over to him, and Fritz entered silently with a cloth.

"Damn the bottles," said Georges, and there was general agreement as Tania took the cloth and wiped the blood away. "Have you any gauze?" she asked, and I told her there was some in the bathroom.

Georges said he'd get it himself, that he was all right, and he walked out to clean up. Lupa sat in the chair Georges had vacated, where he'd gone to inspect the bottle, while the rest of us reassembled ourselves. Marcel said something conciliatory to Henri, and they retired to what had been the American corner. Tania and I went back to the divan, and Paul stood joking with Fritz about his wisdom.

When Fritz had finished cleaning up the spilled beer, he went to get another, and Paul turned and sat with us. "So much for that toast," he said.

Forgoing the next one, we all reached for our beers and drank. Henri and Lupa drained their glasses, and Henri had just yelled in through the kitchen for Fritz to bring more than one more, when Marcel stood up straight, grabbing his throat. He croaked out, "I feel . . ." but before he could finish, he reeled forward over the small table onto his face. Lupa

was to him in a flash, rolling him over and lifting his eyelids.
Georges came back to the door in time to hear him say,
"He's dead."

■ ■ ■

The events of the next moments were confused and rapid,
though they seemed to me to follow one another with ago-
nizing slowness. Tania, sitting next to me, put down her glass
and stared, then covering her face with her hands cried, "Oh
God, no!" and leaned back. I was aware of Georges stopping
in the doorway, gauze over his recent cut, turning pale and
being the second one to reach Marcel's side. Lupa had turned
him over onto his back and undone his collar, but it was too
late. Georges slapped the corpse several times, saying, "Marcel!" over and over in a scolding tone, then looked over to
me as Lupa finally stopped him.

"What happened?" he asked.

Fritz came to the door as I stood to cross the room, and I
told him to take the car to town and get the police. Paul and
Henri stood where they had been sitting and watched in
stunned silence. I walked to where Marcel lay and felt for his
pulse. There was none.

"Get back! Get away!" I yelled at Lupa and Georges. Paul
had gone out to the hall for his coat, and he returned, placing it over Marcel's head. Georges limped back and forth
across the room, hands thrust deep in his pockets. Tania had
stopped crying and stood by the settee. Everything began
moving at normal speed again, and everyone began talking at
once. I went back to Tania and sat next to her, watching the
others. Finally Lupa, who had been sitting, stood again and

bellowed out, "Silence!" and we obeyed. "Let us sit," he said, "and wait for the police."

"Who are you to tell us what to do?" demanded Henri, who seemed quite shaken. Georges, standing next to him, put his arm around his shoulder. Paul sat alone by the fire, looking at the flames.

"But before I do, I will say that while you are all free to move about in town, no one is to leave Valence for any period of time without checking with the authorities."

"But I don't live in Valence," said Paul. "I'm from St. Etienne."

"In that case, monsieur, we will escort you to your home by way of the St. Etienne constabulatory, and you will report to them."

While we waited to be called to the kitchen for questioning, Tania and I sat without a word on the divan, her arm linked into mine. She seemed too calm, almost to the point of breaking, as though she were under some unbearable pressure. Undoubtedly this local tragedy had turned her thoughts to her sons at the front.

The inspector first called Lupa, then Georges, Paul, Henri, Tania, and Fritz. The first four were led to the back door and excused, while Tania and Fritz waited in the kitchen after their questioning. The inspector interrogated me in the front room.

"Monsieur Magiot sends his compliments."

I nodded.

"I've made no arrests. Have you any suspicions?"

"No."

"I'm inclined to think of suicide. He was your close friend, was he not? Had he been unduly depressed?"

It went on in that vein for several minutes. I had no information for him, and he had formed no suspicions himself. He thought it odd that so few of my guests had been French, and asked me about it.

I shrugged. "They are my friends."

· 4 ·

I had supposed that Jacques Magiot, an old acquaintance of mine and the chief of police, would have come out for the investigation, but he sent a young inspector and two gendarmes, who made it clear that their chief's appearance was by no means necessary for the gathering of evidence. The *flics* stationed themselves by the door while the inspector walked around inspecting. He leaned down and sniffed the rug where the beer had spilled.

"Prussic acid," he said.

"Some form of cyanide, at any rate," I answered.

He nodded. "Are you familiar with poisons?"

"Oh come. The almond smell is distinctive."

He noted something in his book.

The others stood about nervously. The inspector spent a bit of time looking at a spiderweblike impression on the coffee table and after a series of "ahems" said that he'd like to question each of us separately.

Finally, a little after midnight, they left. Tania and Fritz came back to join me, and we sat drinking brandy for a time, pensive. The undertaker had come earlier, and my thoughts went back to Marcel's body being removed. I closed my eyes and tried to imagine how he had been only that morning, but I could not. Perhaps it was better that way. I couldn't think of him as a dead man yet. He was the friend of my childhood, and he was gone.

Tania and I went up to bed, leaving the room empty save for Fritz, who sat at the edge of one of the coffee tables, fists clenched and eyes glassy.

■ ■ ■

I awoke while it was still dark and silently got up. The house was oppressive. I needed to get away for a time.

Two days before, the Rue St. Philip had been warming to a new day as I had walked down it to meet Lupa for the first time. Now, at four thirty in the morning, with a light rain falling—still falling, I should say— it gave no hint that it could ever be a pleasant street. The cobblestones were slick and too widely spaced, and twice I nearly fell. It wasn't cold, but the wet darkness kept me shivering.

I'd taken the bottle of cognac and headed for La Couronne, planning to see Lupa in the morning, resolving to enlist his aid. It was not professional. It was not even . . .

That didn't matter. I had to do something about my friend's death. At that moment, I wasn't a professional, and I didn't care.

The tables at La Couronne were chained in place, but the chairs had been moved inside for the night, so I pulled up an

empty fruit crate and sat by the restaurant's front door, leaning back against the building. With my coat, I performed the
futile gesture of wiping the beaded drops from the table,
though it was still raining. There was a small gaslight from
within, and its slight glare fell across the table. The rain was
so fine that it seemed to hang in the air. There was no wind.

I hadn't been seated more than a minute when the door
behind me opened and I found myself facing Lupa.

"Monsieur Giraud, would you care to come inside where
it's dry?"

I noticed that I was, indeed, very wet, and got up and followed him into the bar. He sat on a stool and looked at me
without a word until I spoke.

"I'm surprised to find you awake," I said.

"I was thinking about your friend."

"Yes. I wanted to speak to you about it."

"I don't understand," he said, standing and going around
the bar. He poured himself a beer.

"I think you do."

He took a long draft. "Come downstairs," he said finally.
He opened the door to the kitchen, and we descended.

"May I take your coat?" he asked. "I'm sorry, sir, but I
neglect my manners. I am on edge. Come, let me take your
coat. Do sit down."

We'd entered another room behind the kitchen. It was
warmly lit and pleasant. Three of the walls were covered with
tapestries of a cheap variety, and there were several bookshelves and assorted stuffed chairs. I took one of them.

"I live here," he explained. "You are now my guest. Would
you care for some heated milk? Coffee?"

I looked carefully at this man who had been changed so completely by the act of my coming into his living quarters. He went into some other rooms to deposit the coat, then back to the kitchen, evidently to prepare the milk. For nearly a quarter of an hour I sat while he moved back and forth, bringing first the milk, then a pair of pajamas that he insisted I change into, though they were much too large, then a warm housecoat in which I wrapped myself. He stoked the fire, and before long we were sitting comfortably in silence.

"Now," he said after a time, "what is it that you think I understand?"

I smiled. "I am not a fool, Monsieur Lupa. I am older than you, and perhaps not as naturally gifted, but I have been in my business—perhaps I should say 'our' business—for over twenty years, and I have learned a few things. My efforts have been checked and checked again since coming to Valence, and I feel that yours have been likewise. I think we should work together."

"Indeed," he said. "I didn't know you'd worked as a chef." Suddenly he chuckled. "Of course, I jest. I thought it would be necessary that we work together, but I wanted to be sure of you, and certain of your superiors were less than rapturous in their recommendations."

I bridled somewhat and spoke in clipped tones. "You may be sure of me."

"I know that. I have been satisfied. But have you? Can you be sure of me?"

My head was swimming with cognac and fatigue, and yet I immediately perceived the import of the question. Here, indeed, was a Rubicon of sorts, and I must either cast my die with this man or count him as an enemy. There was, there could be, no middle ground.

And what, in fact, did I know of him beyond the briefs, the hearsay, the professional reports that—and no one knew this as well as I—often hid as much as they revealed?

He was an agent. Of that there was no doubt. I was reasonably sure that he didn't work for the Germans, but could I be as certain that he was committed, as I was, to the interests of France? Before hostilities had erupted, Europe had been a checkerboard of conflicting states, and even now, with the combatants clearly defined, only a fool would suppose that the goals of England, for example, everywhere coincided with those of France. Where did Lupa stand?

I felt his eyes boring into my own as his question hung in the room, and yet he didn't seem inclined to press. Could I be sure of him?

The answer, of course, had to be no. We were both agents at war, trained to trust no one. Hadn't Lupa been sitting in Marcel's seat just before he'd been poisoned? But then another thought occurred to me: it really wasn't my decision to make. I'd been ordered to find and work with Lupa. I didn't have to trust or respect my superiors, but as a soldier I had to obey them.

And there was another point: I had already revealed myself to the younger man. If he was not to be trusted, then my usefulness here in Valence was at an end. Now my own vulnerability, here in Lupa's quarters, could become my own best test of his credibility. Simply put, if I were alive in the morning, he would have proven himself worthy of my confidence. It may not have been the most professional of solutions, but in my wearied state it made a great deal of sense.

One final consideration, even more unprofessional, forced itself into my consciousness. With Marcel dead, perhaps I simply needed to trust someone to fill the hole he had left. With more instinct than reason, I felt Lupa to be the man for that role.

"I have to believe in you," I said at last. "I have no choice."

He sipped at his beer and stared into the fire. Quite some time passed. "I suspect everyone," he said finally.

A wave of regret over the loss of my friend passed over me. "Please," I said. "I need your help." He started to blur before me as fatigue set in. I put my hand over my eyes and felt his come to rest on my shoulder.

"Come," he said, "we'll talk in the morning."

He took me back to his quarters, down a hall that seemed to be a dead end. He put down a mattress on the floor and brought a thick blanket for it.

"Let us be careful," he said almost gently. We were by now speaking in the familiar. "We're going to be needing each other." I lay down and blew out the candle beside me. He retreated a few steps, then stopped. "Do you mind if I call you Jules?"

"No."

"Satisfactory." Another pause. "I am very sorry."

■ ■ ■

I slept for seven hours. When I woke up, my clothes had been sent out and already returned, so I dressed and walked back out to the kitchen. No one was there. I went outside and found Lupa on the sidewalk finishing his beer. It was still drizzling, but the awning had been pulled.

"Did you sleep well?" he asked.

I felt miserable, so I merely grunted. He ordered me a *petite calva*; and I drank it off quickly.

"Have you been awake long?" I asked.

"Since eight o'clock." I must have looked at him in disbelief, for he continued, "A schedule that may be whimsically broken is no schedule at all. In the end the logical order one tries to impose on one's life is sacrificed to quotidian cares. Even this beer," he said, motioning to the brew, "though it doesn't compare to yours, helps in its way to reestablish the order that last night destroyed."

I thought he was being peevish, so I said nothing. He looked at me and smiled, emptying his glass. "Come with me, Jules. I have an appointment."

We went back down to his quarters, which seemed smaller than they had been in the early morning, or even a half hour before. The hall I'd slept in was off to the left of the sitting room, but we crossed over to a door at the right and into a rather large office. The right-hand wall was covered with pots and pans, costly copper and cast iron, while the left sported a picture of Dreyfus and, somewhat incongruously, a bull's ear. Behind the desk was another of the cheap tapestries that he used to cover the bare rock wall. His entire quarters seemed to be a type of bunker—certainly nothing like the typical cellar one finds around here.

He walked to the corner nearest the bull's ear—a memento from Spain, I later learned—and lifted away the tapestry, showing a large hole opening into blackness, into which he stepped, motioning for me to follow. He lit a tallow and we moved through a narrow, high cave for several hundred meters. So this was where he disappeared to in the afternoons. I wondered where the cave would come out.

"Handy having all the limestone around here," he said. "It took comparatively little work to finish this passage after I arrived here."

I found that difficult to believe, though I knew that some of the natural caves in the region extended for incredible distances. In the end, the cave proved to be nearly a kilometer in length, and I was totally unprepared for where it abutted. Lupa pulled aside another bit of rug and stepped into a cellar of amazing fragrance.

"Where are we?" I asked. The smell alone had nearly driven away my headache.

He seemed almost playful as he leaned back against a waist-high bench. He held the candle out behind him, and I could make out rows and rows of flowers. He breathed deeply.

"Marvelous," he said. "It always affects me."

Then quickly he straightened up again and moved to a door, which led to a stairway, which in turn opened into a well-lighted planting room. There was a partition in front of the door, and we waited behind it while Lupa peeked out to see who was in the shop. When he was satisfied, we walked out. A woman, about thirty, with dark hair and features, stood talking with a man whose back was toward us as we approached. Lupa went up to the woman, kissed her on the cheek, and said something to her in a language I didn't understand—and I speak five languages. She disappeared to where we'd been.

"Watkins."

"Hello."

The two men embraced and began speaking in English.

"Where have you sent Anna?" asked the stranger.

"She forgot to turn on the cellar lights again. The plants will surely die. I'm glad you're here. We've had problems."

"I've heard already. Routier's been killed. No clues. You were there. Who did it?"

The man was in his twenties and would have looked perfectly nondescript except for the great swelling in his left cheek. His hair was short and brown, his suit common, and he wore no tie. Occasionally he chewed at his cheek.

"I haven't much of an idea," said Lupa. "It could have been any of us. Oh, excuse me, this is Jules Giraud. Joseph Watkins."

We shook hands as the woman returned.

"Look at his cheek, will you?" she said. "Those damned olives again."

Watkins grinned crookedly. "Addicted," he said. "Can't get enough of the blasted things."

"He's been horrible all morning," said the woman. "Eating so many of them he can't talk, spitting the pits wherever he happens to be. I should have tossed him out long ago. If he wasn't so . . ." She smiled and touched his arm. He moved aside. "Hello," she said, crossing to me, "my name is Anna Dubrov. I've seen you before in town."

I nodded. "Jules Giraud."

Lupa suggested we go to the back of the shop. On the way, Watkins leaned over one of the potted plants and straightened up again without the swelling in his cheek. He was grinning broadly.

"Anyone care for an olive?" he asked, taking ten or fifteen from his coat pocket. When no one responded, he deposited the entire handful into his mouth.

Lupa stood with an arm around Anna, waiting for this frivolous Englishman to finish chewing. When the pits had been stuffed into his cheek, Lupa began.

"Any news?"

"Yes, and specific." Once he started talking, he was entirely businesslike. Perhaps he wasn't as frivolous as he seemed.

"Continue."

"Well, naturally you're here on your own affairs, something about assassinations and so forth, but I thought—"

"You can drop that," said Lupa. "M. Giraud, as you know, is an agent of the French, and he is now in our confidence." He turned to me, continuing, "I am a free operative working for the English government. I know all this has been denied time and again in your inquiries about me. You know how that is. My uncle is a nonambulatory genius whom I detest, but he is probably the most important man in England, and we share some views during wartime."

"So you work for England?"

"For the time being, yes, but I direct my own inquiries."

"By the way," said Watkins, "Altamont says—"

"That will do," Lupa said abruptly. "Let us get on with your information."

"Yes, well, um . . ." He fumbled a moment, then leaned over and spit out the pits. "We've got information that he is not here for assassination. You're aware of the arms and mu-nitions factory at St. Etienne?"

Lupa's gaze was withering.

Watkins pressed on. "It's going to be blown."

I found myself smiling. "How do you know?"

"One of the boys flushed a Kraut spy and persuaded him to drop a few tidbits, and this was one of them. Unfortu-nately, our man brought some friends. They all got a bit car-ried away during the interrogation, and the Kraut died before he could be of much more use."

Lupa looked at me. "And they say that we are fighting the barbarians." To Watkins: "Did you get any descriptions, any-thing definite?"

"Not of your man, no. But there was something."

"What was that?"

"It's to be an inside job."

I laughed, and the man looked at me angrily.

"What's funny, mate?"

"I'm sorry," I said, "but it would have to be. Have you seen the place? It's guarded rather completely."

Lupa was absently running his fingers through some dirt in a pot next to him. He seemed lethargically calm until he spoke, at which time he fired his questions at the other man.

"Where was he caught?"

"Marseilles. Usual narcotics stuff. He was delivering to their man in St. Etienne."

"Why didn't the fools let him deliver?"

"I think you've answered your own question. The fool—that is, our man—wanted to make sure he didn't escape. They knew something big was going on in this area. He wanted to get a piece of it."

"And lose the pie in the bargain." Lupa was annoyed, and I could see why.

"One other thing bothers me," Watkins said.

"What's that?"

"I think he *is* here to assassinate. That is patently a part of it. Remember, we have had—what is it now?—three deaths of operatives in the past year. It's just a hypothesis, but it is corroborated by the lack of any other overt activity until he moves. That's all. Of course, no clues. But the man must sooner or later make a mistake. He must."

He shrugged and reached into his pocket for some more olives. Someone walked into the store and Anna went to the front. Lupa pulled up a stool and sat down. He seemed completely engrossed in the plant beside him. Suddenly he looked up and spoke.

"I hope you're right. Because if he is only here to blow the factory, then when the job is done, he'll disappear. Whereas if he is here for a dual purpose, one job may give us the clue to the other."

"You think he's the man who killed Routier?" asked Watkins.

"Do you think he isn't?"

"Then he must have been . . ."

"Precisely," Lupa said, "he must have been among our gathering last night."

I started to object. After all, everyone who had been there was a friend. But even as I began my defense, I realized that there was no other conclusion.

"That's good," Watkins said. "It narrows the field considerably."

"Yes," Lupa agreed. "Yes, it does."

He got up and beckoned me to follow him. He paused at the screen to the back door. "Joseph, you'll have to go to St. Etienne."

Anna turned around to wave good-bye, and we proceeded back through the cellar, which was now brightly lit and stunning in color as well as fragrance. Another walk through the tunnel, and we reappeared in Lupa's rooms.

I sat across from him. The weight of my friend's death had begun to settle on me again. I must have looked tired.

"What are your ideas?" Lupa had gone to an oversize, over-stuffed chair. "I'd like a beer," he said, but he didn't get up.

"I'd like some sleep," I said. We spoke in English.

"I'd say you need it. But first, what do you think of St. Etienne and our list of suspects?"

"That's been bothering me," I said. "I mean the fact that it looks like the man we're after is a friend of mine. Going on that assumption, everyone has a plausible opportunity, but . . ." I stopped.

He grunted. "It begins to look that way."

"More than you know," I said.

I got up, walked out to the kitchen and up the stairs, ordered two beers at the bar, and returned. He nodded graciously when I handed him a bottle, and took a long drink.

"I detest drinking beer from a bottle, but what can one do?" He drank again. "More than I know?"

"List our suspects," I said. "Paul Anser lives in St. Etienne. Georges Lavoie delivers there, as does Henri Pulis—I would assume even to the arsenal itself. Georges with his first-aid supplies and Henri, of course, with his food. It's one of those newfangled buildings where the workers have their own cafeteria and medical facility. I've heard Tania talk about it."

"Tania?"

"That's the worst part."

He finished his beer and waited.

"One of Tania's oldest acquaintances, through her husband, who was a French officer . . . Anyway, one of their friends was Maurice Ponty, who happens to be the director of the St. Etienne arms factory. She still sees him about once a month."

Lupa leaned back in his chair and sighed deeply. "That's everyone."

"Except Fritz."

"No, not except Fritz."

"You have something on him," I asked, "some connection?"

Lupa shook his head. "I was loath to consider him because of his cooking. He is so *sympathetique*. Still, that is a flaw in my own method."

"But you just said you have nothing on him."

"Nothing definite, Jules, but certainly something. It stretches the bounds of coincidence that every one of your guests has some foreign connection. Until I have satisfied myself with Fritz's references in Germany before the war began, I have to include him among the suspects. I have a man working on it now."

"But what possible . . . ?" I began.

"Jules, please. I must suspect everyone."

"Even me?"

He was young. A look of ineffable sadness crossed his countenance. "I'm afraid, my new friend, even you."

I stood up. "The beer is terrible, but it isn't that. I must be getting on home. Would you like me to have Fritz send up a case of my beer, if it wouldn't spook you?"

"That would be excellent," he said, lifting the corners of his mouth in what perhaps he thought was a broad smile.

"Meanwhile, I'll get some sleep and then try and contact everyone and see what I can find."

Lupa seemed to consider something, then stopped me from leaving by raising his hand. "Jules," he said, "a small point, but in English the word 'contact' should never be used as a verb."

"*Au revoir,*" I replied with dignity, then turned on my heels, left him, and began walking home through the gray and dismal afternoon.

■ ■ ■

Stones crunched noisily under my feet as I trudged homeward, the sound a somber coda to the theme playing over and over in my mind. Lupa had said, "I must suspect everyone," and he was right. I walked slowly, hands deep in my pockets, head down.

Everyone . . .

I thought of the word as a sledgehammer pounding into the wall of reluctance I had built against suspicion of my friends. And they had been my friends, every one of them. Now, until this was all over, they would not be friends, and they might never be again.

I remembered how it had all begun, with Paul Anser. It had been in Paris around 1911. What had he been doing there? Ah yes, publishing something. He did actually publish poetry. I had two or three of his bound collections and even an autographed manuscript at the house. There had been a party, I recall, with lots of young men from London taking the Grand Tour, as well as several charming young women. I had the feeling that I'd been asked to chaperon, but that suited me. The crowd was lively and intelligent, a far cry from the stultifying soirees held by the wives of military men to further their husbands' careers.

Paul had been the entertainment, or part of it, and he was well received. Afterward, though, when most of the younger set had paired off, I had seen him standing alone, looking rather at sea, and I took pity on him. His command of French then was not so good as it has become, and we spoke English, discovering to our mutual delight that we were neighbors. When he had returned to Valence several weeks later, he had called on me while Marcel had been visiting, and we'd had such a good time drinking beer, and—significantly?—talking politics that we all decided to make a regular event of it.

So it had been Paul, Marcel, and me from the start. Seen from a certain perspective, and one that I had truthfully never considered until this moment, it had been, or could have been, a most fertile field for espionage. Back in the beginning, we'd all shared the common confidences of newfound friends. Had it all been masterful grilling on Paul's part?

I thought back. I had aired my disagreements over policy rather freely. Marcel had done the same. To the extent that Paul had been fascinated, hanging on our words, we had felt flattered, viewing him with friendly condescension. Those naive, neutral, isolationist Americans, we had thought. Now I bitterly recast the litany in my mind: we naive, romantic, gullible French!

Dark rain clouds scudded against the overcast sky. I had been wandering, lost in contemplation. Though Valence wasn't a particularly large city, I found myself in an unknown neighborhood as a light drizzle began to fall. Ancient houses leaned threateningly over narrow stone streets. I considered turning around, trying to retrace my route, but since I'd been paying no attention whatever, I realized that I was truly lost. Turning back wouldn't help. There was nothing to do but continue walking, hoping I would stumble upon some familiar landmark.

Everyone . . .

Henri had been the next. It had come about naturally enough, since I bought my beer-making supplies from his shop. I remember the first time we'd gotten into a discussion of technique. He had a particularly dependable supplier of excellent German hops. German hops! His interest was so genuine, his personality so forthright, that I had spontaneously decided to ask him around.

And he became the most regular of the guests. His attendance was never in doubt, which, now that I thought of it, was provocative. With a wife and a large family as well as a prospering business, he might have been expected to have the most demands on his time. Instead, our weekly gatherings were obviously a matter of great priority to him.

Why, just the past night he'd left his wife in the middle of a disagreement, as Lupa had pointed out. Were our beer meetings more important to him than his domestic harmony? And if they were, why?

Again I reflected on his bluff exterior—a happy, life-loving Greek. And the more I thought on it, the more incongruous were his business successes and his easy camaraderie with our varied and rather highbrow group.

A dead-end street brought me up short. I was just as content to be lost—the physical disorientation matched my mental turmoil. I was losing faith in the world I lived in—a world where my friends were not as they seemed, where love and trust might be bargaining chips, and duplicity the coin of the realm.

Everyone . . .

I could not have met Georges more innocuously. Late last summer, just after I'd come down here, I was returning from a bit of business in St. Etienne in my motorcar when I came upon a well-dressed limping figure hitchhiking on the roadway. New to the area, Georges had miscalculated the distances between a few of his sales calls in St. Etienne and so had missed his train back to Valence. During the drive, we struck up a fascinating discussion on the question of reincarnation, and I sensed that he would fit in perfectly among my beer guests. And so it had proved.

And yet there were coincidences that a mind more suspicious than my own might not have overlooked. That first Wednesday meeting with Georges in attendance was also Marcel's first day back in the area. In other words, it was within two weeks of our first operative's death. And that of course meant that Georges's arrival in Valence occurred within days of that "accident." Further, of all of our number, he had the

least history. I had known of, or had references to account
for, each of my other friends, each of the other suspects.

Finally, and more subjectively, I have had a great deal of
experience with members of my profession, and if there can
be said to be a "type" of mind in the field, Georges's most
neatly fit that category—heavily reliant on facts, possessed of
enough originality to deduce from those facts (Marcel's glaring flaw and Lupa's forte), plus a certain glibness, a way of
getting by on the surface of events while chaos reigns on the
operative level.

The psychological babble was fine in its place, and yet the
fact remained that Georges had not even been in the same
room when Marcel had taken his last draft. And no service in
the world would hire a man with Georges's limp—it was
simply unheard of.

A recognizable square loomed ahead of me in the drizzle,
and I found myself suddenly almost too dispirited to keep
moving toward it. What was the point of going home? What,
indeed, was home? Another hollow concept such as loyalty,
duty, honor—all fine words to fight and die over, but nothing to take too seriously.

But the old discipline directed my footsteps just as my
training led my thoughts back to the issue. The stakes here
were nothing less than survival, and sentiment must be viewed
only as a dangerous luxury, an enemy as deadly as any I would
ever face.

Everyone . . .

How could Fritz have lived in my house for a year without causing me a moment of suspicion? And yet who was
more ideally suited to keep tabs on my movements and re-

port on them? No one had had a better opportunity to place poison in Marcel's bottle, except of course Lupa, who had been sitting in that seat. But my trust in Lupa had proven itself well grounded. Or had it? Perhaps he'd kept me alive last night for another, future purpose. Perhaps in some other game, I was a bishop and Marcel a quickly expendable pawn— perhaps and maybe and again perhaps. My mind was beginning to reel with uncertainties, with possibilities.

Everyone . . .

And even Tania . . .

No! Not Tania! Not the only woman I had ever loved. It was unthinkable. Even if it killed me, I would not suspect her. I shook my head, trying as best I could to purge the poisonous thought . . .

. . . and looked up to find myself in the middle of the square, still confused and lonelier than I had ever felt before.

■ ■ ■

The rain became fierce, and again I found myself soaked. In no mood to continue an already disagreeable walk, I hired a carriage back to my home. Fritz greeted me at the door with undisguised concern, tempered with reproval.

"Are you well, sir?"

"Damn it, Fritz, no. No, I'm not well. I'm drenched, my clothes are ruined for the second time, I'm tired, and my oldest friend has been murdered in my house. No, I'm not well at all."

He stood back and silently took my clothes.

"I'm sorry to snap," I said, "but it has been a trying time."

"Monsieur Lupa came by this morning and told me you

were in good hands. Madame Chessal went home after breakfast. Would you like some tea or brandy?"

He handed me my robe, and I went into the front room to sit before the fire, where I brooded for a while about my age until Fritz came back with tea laced with brandy. After one cup I fell off to sleep.

Fritz woke me again when it was already dark, served me a small meal of coddled eggs with sherry and black butter, and suggested I retire, which I did.

· 5 ·

Ironically, but predictably, the sun blazed forth on Friday morning for Marcel's funeral, and found me well rested. Fritz always rose at dawn and, when the weather permitted, breakfasted by himself in the arbor. Since I was rarely awake by then, he justly considered this his time, and I was loath to disturb him, so I poured myself a cup of espresso before walking out. I was ashamed of myself for the way I'd acted the day before. These days at home had weakened me. I resolved to shake myself out of this softness.

I walked to the arbor in my robe and bare feet, enjoying the feel of the wet grass. Fritz sat on a cushion that he'd brought out for the stone bench, eating a brioche with some ripe Brie and drinking his coffee. Already, at seven o'clock, the chill had gone from the air. The house and arbor had a striking, newly washed quality. A slight mist rose from the shingles of the roof.

"Good morning, Fritz. Don't get up. No muffins for me. I'll just be having coffee in the mornings for a while."

We sat for a while without speaking. The stream murmured peacefully. At such a time it was hard to imagine the trenches, the carnage, a Europe—perhaps soon a world—at war. Yet it would be fatal to be lulled, to allow oneself to forget.

Fritz pulled me from my reverie after he'd drained his cup. "You're going to the funeral?"

"Yes, of course."

"Madame Chessal, then, asks if you'll pick her up on the way."

In a half hour, I had dressed and gone to the old servants' quarters, where I kept my automobile, a Ford from America that I'd been allowed to keep after mobilization, though there'd been a substantial and very local "tax" for the privilege. The car started without any problem, and within minutes I pulled up to Tania's house. She sat out on the front patio of the long, light blue structure, nibbling halfheartedly at her croissant.

"Good morning," I said.

She stood quickly and came over to embrace me. She looked tired.

"But you," she said, "where did you go that Monsieur Lupa wound up taking care of you? Are you all right?"

I patted her shoulder. "I'm fine. I think I just needed to forget, or perhaps to remember. At any rate, to lay Marcel to rest. I'm perfectly well now. Come, are you ready? You don't look as though you've had such a wonderful night yourself."

She took my arm, leaning a fragrant head for a moment

against my shoulder. She sighed. "Sometimes we're so alike it's frightening. I couldn't stop thinking about poor Marcel. Last night I'm afraid I drank rather too much wine. Danielle had to put me to bed."

"Fritz did the same for me."

We got into the car and drove to the cemetery. The service wasn't due to begin until ten o'clock, so we had nearly two hours to walk through the surrounding countryside and compose ourselves. I decided that my suspicions about Tania on the day before had been ridiculous, but resolved not to say anything unnecessary to anyone until this mess had been cleared up.

When we finally walked down to the cemetery proper, Georges and Paul had arrived. Paul looked especially out of place in a dark suit. In the time that I'd known him, I couldn't ever recall having seen him dressed even semiformally before. We joined them by the gate.

Gradually, some other of Marcel's friends and relatives began to appear, and the four of us who had been in the room that night found ourselves effectively ostracized. Henri and his wife arrived among a small group who left them immediately after they'd passed the gate. Madame Pulis, whom I'd never met, was weeping, and Tania walked over to comfort her. Henri joined the rest of us.

After a few moments of uncomfortable small talk, we walked over to the grave. Marcel's parents had died long ago, and he hadn't been married. I had probably been his closest friend, and yet the others around the grave treated all of us as though we'd been his enemies. We stood in a knot while the usual forms were followed and, when the body had been lowered, were the first to turn and go. Madame Pulis had been constantly crying throughout.

Georges walked crookedly next to me. "Rather ugly, wasn't it?"

"Yes," I said, "but I don't suppose you can blame them."

Gathered around my car, we stopped to talk. Tania packed Madame Pulis into their carriage and walked pensively back. "I can't understand those people," she said. "Henri, your wife . . ." She stopped.

"I know, I know. I suppose I shouldn't've brought her along. She's so emotional. She was fine until we met that other group. They asked if I'd been there Wednesday and acted as if . . . well, you know. And she's very sensitive to that sort of thing. You'd think one of us killed him, the way they were acting."

Paul was seated on the running board, his tie now off, his coat across his legs. "It appears," he said, "that one of us did."

"Well, I didn't," stormed Henri. "I goddamn well didn't!"

"I didn't say you did, Henri. Calm down. But it isn't un-reasonable to assume that one of us planted that poison now, is it? You might as easily assume that I did it."

I looked sharply at him.

Georges spoke up. "Have the police mentioned to any of you their suspicions? Motives, hints, clues?"

Everyone said no.

"The point is, they mentioned to me . . . well, we shouldn't go around picking each other to pieces. They mentioned that it seemed to them to be at least as good a bet that it was suicide."

"That's absurd," I said. "I'd been with him most of the day. He hadn't been depressed. In fact, he'd been looking forward to the summer."

"Well, the alternative, of course," said Paul, standing up, "is that one of us did it."

"Again, not necessarily," said Georges.

"What do you mean?"

"Not necessarily one of us. One of 'us' isn't here."

"Lupa!" said Henri.

"It does seem strange he didn't come," said Tania, "though some people simply cannot abide funerals."

Paul laughed. "No one likes funerals."

"My wife does." Henri shook his head, and we all laughed as the tension broke. "Speaking of . . ." He smiled at all of us and began to walk to the carriage. Tania called after him and asked if she might go with him, since I'd told her that I had business in St. Etienne.

The three of us remaining watched them move off slowly, and I asked Paul if he needed a lift. Georges said he had some deliveries to make at St. Etienne and would I mind if he accompanied us? Since he had to pick up his supplies, we all agreed to meet later in the afternoon, and I drove off alone toward La Couronne. On the way, I remembered the beer I'd promised Lupa and detoured back by way of my home.

Chez moi, I changed into something more comfortable and asked Fritz if he'd mind arranging the delivery of several cases of the beer to Lupa. Since it was lunchtime, Fritz insisted I stay and have something to eat, and he quickly prepared a small plate of ham croquettes, fresh bread, and a delicious paté made, he said, from the liver of a wild hare. Since he didn't hunt, I had reason to doubt him, though one of the neighborhood boys might have come around with his catch. Still, wild hare or not, it was excellent. I had one of my own beers to overcome my lurking fear about them, and during the first few sips, Fritz looked at me with real anxiety. I smiled.

"They don't produce cyanide of themselves," I said.

He didn't think that at all funny and crossed back into the house, where he could eat in his cool and shaded kitchen, washing everything down with his daily *demi-bouteille* of un-complicated wine.

I decided it would be a waste of time to see Lupa before I'd been to St. Etienne, and so I found myself for the second time that day with some spare time on my hands. I walked slowly up the stairs to my room and reached into the false bottom of my lower left-hand drawer, taking out my pistol.

It was an older but nevertheless effective weapon, excel-lent for close quarters and concealment. I don't know why I'd stopped wearing it when I'd returned home this last time. That had been foolish. It was a derringer, its tiny butt over-laid with carved ivory. For all its beauty, it was a terribly powerful weapon—the same gun, though of course an ear-lier model, had been used to assassinate the American Presi-dent Lincoln. I carried it in a special holster that I wore under my shirt. Up in my room, I began to clean and oil its few moving parts, so that by the time I left the house, I felt finally prepared for the work I might have to do.

It was still early for our rendezvous—I was meeting my friends at the town fountain at one thirty—so I stopped by

Tania's house to see if she'd come back yet. I found her inside, fuming. Sitting down next to her, I kissed her on the cheek.

"Is something wrong?"

"That man is such a . . ." She was so angry her voice was shaking. "And I thought you were to be in St. Etienne."

I explained the delay, though her eyes still flashed in anger. "It's not really you—it's him. He's so infuriating, I . . ."

"Now, now," I continued, "Henri's under a lot of pressure, and . . ."

"Not Henri. That other man, the one you asked to join us the other night. Lupa!" She stood up and stalked around the room.

"What's he done?"

She stopped and glared across at me. Then suddenly her face softened, and she walked back and kissed me.

"I'm sorry. I'm just very upset. Let's go outside and talk, shall we?"

So we walked out to where she'd eaten earlier that morning. She asked Danielle to bring us some tea, then sat down.

"Now," I said, "what's wrong? What's Lupa done?"

"He's done nothing. He's just so arrogant! He omits doing things, and so superciliously . . . well, no: I'm being hysterical." She leaned forward and clasped her hands together on the table.

"We were coming back, and as you know, Madame Pulis was very upset by the whole thing, and I was thinking of the callousness of our fellow townspeople. We happened to pass La Couronne on our way, and we saw your Monsieur Lupa sitting under the awning, reading a newspaper and drinking beer. I wanted to scold him—all right, I know I'm too much a mother sometimes—but I did want to. I asked Henri to stop.

"Now," she continued, stopping me before I could interrupt, "don't think I was going to snap at him for missing the funeral. After all, I realized that he hardly knew Marcel. I was just angry. I really don't know why I stopped. Perhaps I was being too whimsical. But nevertheless, I did it. Henri let me out and I walked over and asked if he'd mind if I joined him for a moment. Do you know what he said?"

I smiled. "I'd guess he said something like, 'To be frank with you, yes, I would mind.' "

"Well, of course, he wasn't that rude, but I certainly wasn't made to feel very welcome. After I'd sat down, he carefully ignored me while he finished the column he was reading, drank off his beer, called for the waiter, and ordered two more. Finally, he looked straight at me, and in the sweetest voice asked if I'd like some refreshment.

"I asked for a café au lait, and he appeared to shudder slightly as he ordered. I asked him if something was wrong, if he'd rather I left.

" 'No,' he said, 'I simply have a prejudice against milk and coffee together in the same cup. Two tolerable beverages by themselves, but together,' and here he turned his mouth up the smallest degree, 'together rather like a man and a woman who individually are pleasant but who fail as a couple.' So we sat in silence until the waiter returned."

Danielle came back with the tea, and we poured.

"I still fail to see, my dear," I said, "what he's done to so upset you. I grant you that he's arrogant and outspoken, but not without a certain charm."

"Well, he's not learned to polish his charms, so they appear cheap."

"All right, now, what else?"

She sipped at her tea. "As soon as the waiter had gone he looked at me in all politeness. 'And now, madame, what can I do for you? You look a bit tired.'

" 'I am a bit tired,' I said. 'One of my dearest friends was buried this morning.'

" 'Yes?' he answered, as if to say, 'Well, so what?'

"By this time I was so rattled that I'm afraid I rather blurted, 'We were wondering why you hadn't bothered to attend the funeral.'

" 'We?'

" 'Yes, we. Those of us who'd been at Jules's. We were all there, as was proper. Except, of course, for you.'

"He picked up his beer and drank as though completely dismissing me. I tell you, Jules, I was sorely tempted to slap him. Finally, he put his glass down, told me I was upset, and asked me if I would care to lunch with him. Then he proceeded to speak of his upcoming lunch as though it were all that mattered in the world. I'll try to give you some of the flavor of it."

As she spoke, Tania tried to imitate Lupa's deep baritone: " 'Sausages. I was in Spain a few years ago and one day I was standing outside a tapas bar, and the smell of fresh sausage pulled me inside. A large, smiling woman, Señora Beran, was grilling ten or more sausages behind the bar, and so I sat down and began talking with her. She said the sausages were prepared by her son, Jerome, and the recipe was his special secret, but I was welcome to try them. As soon as I'd tasted them, I knew them to be superb, and the flavor remained with me until, indeed, I could think of nothing else. Daily, I went to this same bar and, I'm afraid, badgered that poor woman to distraction. I had to have that recipe. Finally, though, I had to leave and, since that time, have tried unsuccessfully to duplicate that flavor. I've written to Jerome Beran personally, through his mother, but he's been elusive. So now once each month I try again. Not more often because the frustration of failure is bitter indeed. And I dare to call myself a chef. Ha!' "

She looked down into her tea. The forenoon breeze whipped her shining dark hair intermittently into her eyes. She reached out her hand across the table for me to take it. "Can you imagine, Jules? He sat and talked about that sausage as though there were no war, no deaths . . ." She paused for a moment to control her voice. "Then, when the sausage arrived, he took a bite and immediately removed from his pocket a small notebook and wrote something. 'It's not right,' he said simply. 'I must use less brandy and more fowl.' Thereupon he proceeded to eat every last bit of sausage, pausing at regular intervals to shake his head.

"It was not until he had finished that he addressed himself to me again. 'Now, as to your question, madame. By the way, are you enjoying the sausage? Excellent wine, even though it's Spanish, don't you think?' Food, food, food. All right, the man's a chef, but really, Jules . . ."

I patted her hand.

" 'Why didn't I attend the funeral?' he finally began. 'There are two reasons. Both, I'm afraid, quite selfish. One, I dislike funerals. A man is a man until his death, after which he becomes mere mineral matter. If one is of a cathartic cast, there may be benefit in public interment, but, even then, the catharsis is misdirected. Death is not tragedy but pathos. Two, lately I've been becoming much too flexible in my schedule, and I decided to end that flexibility.' He looked at me as though he'd explained everything."

"He is rather intractable," I offered.

"I was so upset by this time, I didn't know what to do. He sat looking at me from across that small table, seemingly quite pleased with himself. I wanted to leave, but I wanted to, well, to make him mad, so I stood up and said, 'If I were you I'd be a little more careful. More than one of us believes you killed Marcel,' and I turned to go. He spoke my name then, so abruptly that everyone looked up, and I came back to the table.

" 'Let's not be ridiculous,' he said. 'I am an acquaintance of Monsieur Giraud. In fact, I've spoken to him at some length. For now, you are upset, and I suggest you go home and get some rest.'

"With that, he called for a carriage and sent me on my way. What should I think of him, Jules? Is he a friend of yours?"

Of course, Lupa had told her nothing about our real relationship, leaving it to me to make that decision. I'd tried to be honest with Tania as much as possible, though I hadn't told her what I really was. There had been no need. And now, I was reluctant to tell her because I was afraid of her. Afraid that she might not understand or, on the other hand, would understand too well. So I temporized.

"I wouldn't worry about Monsieur Lupa, dear," I said. "I

spent the night at his place on Wednesday after my walking took me downtown. He'd come to the gathering only to try my beer, and was genuinely upset at the way things turned out. He'd only met Marcel that afternoon and they had had no disagreements. They seemed to get on quite well. Certainly, he had no reason to kill him."

"But which of us did?" she asked.

I shrugged. "I really don't know. I don't know." I slumped and stared down at the well-kept gravel of her terrace. "I can't believe he killed himself."

"Maybe Henri is right," she said, "with his rumors."

"What are those?"

"He said that he's heard for the past several months that Marcel had something to do with espionage, with the war."

A chill passed through me. "Henri said that? Where did he hear that?"

"I don't know."

"Well, that's absurd. I've known Marcel all my life, and—"

"But what if he was? What if he was, and another of us is, and we don't know, and he was killed by one of his friends to keep . . . Oh, Jules," she said, "I'm afraid."

I stood up and she rose to embrace me.

"I'm sorry," she said. "I shouldn't be such a baby. It's just with all of this, and the boys away at the front . . . I just don't know what to make of things."

I kissed her, and suddenly she stiffened against me.

"What's that?" she demanded, putting her hand under my arm where I kept my gun.

I had to tell her. "A pistol, just to be safe."

Her lip quivered. She was going to cry. "Jules, please, don't you get mixed up in this. Please."

"Now, now," I said. "I'm not 'mixed up' in anything. I merely felt a little nervous and decided at least to be in a position to protect myself should any of my friends . . ." I trailed off.

She buried her face in my shoulder and cried softly. "Any of your friends. Why won't they leave us alone? Oh, poor Marcel." Her voice broke again. She looked up at me pleadingly. "Jules, really, you're not involved? You're not a spy?"

"No," I said, "no, I'm not a spy. I'm a middle-aged man who's getting old and ready to retire with his lover. I don't want anything to threaten that, so I carry a gun, but only until we find what happened to Marcel. All I want to do is brew beer and tend my vineyards"—I picked up her chin—"and love you."

She smiled bravely.

I kissed her again and stepped back. "I have to go. Georges and Paul will be waiting. I'll pick you up on the way back. We'll stay together tonight."

I watched her walk off into the house, then turned and headed down the stairs to the Ford. The damn thing was, all I really did want to do was brew beer and tend my vineyards and live with Tania. But, then, what if Tania were a spy? No, I wouldn't let myself think that.

It was hot in the car as I turned into the road. I'd have to see Lupa after I'd been to St. Etienne, and I found myself hoping that Fritz would deliver the beer before long. I was as bad as Lupa with his sausages. My rituals were beginning to keep me from the pain of Marcel's death, as a kind of insulation.

But my friend was dead, and when the rituals were over, that would remain, so I drove slowly, thinking of my own best sausage recipe and watching out for potholes.

· 6 ·

The war was everywhere. If normal life can be said to continue in a town stripped of its young men, then normal life went on. But of course the war touched everyone you knew or met and colored the mood of the entire countryside. Even as the sun shone brightly down on our fountain, where Paul sat with his pants rolled up cooling his feet, the streets were cleared for a convoy of trucks and carriages carrying supplies to the front.

I pulled over and parked across the square, watching the vehicles roll past, then walked over to join my friends. Paul was smoking a cigarette and talking animatedly to Georges. They stopped as I drew nearer, and Paul pulled his feet from the water and rolled down his trousers.

"Ready?"

"Yes."

"Let's go, then."

We helped Georges with his packages. There seemed to

be enough gauze for the entire army, but he explained that there was to be a huge shipment to the front with the St. Etienne factory as the central warehousing point. It took several trips but finally we loaded all the bags, and after a *demi* at one of the cafes bordering the square, we left. Paul took particular delight in sitting atop the bundles of gauze. I'd removed the top to the car, and as we drove along he sang off-key but with great enthusiasm. He wanted to forget the funeral as soon as possible.

Finally, when the wind kept blowing his tobacco away before he could roll it, he joined us in the front seat.

"Never had that problem on a horse."

We rode along, then, quietly for a while. The trees passed quickly by on either side of the road. Paul smoked in what he called the "French manner," blowing the smoke out of his mouth and up into his nose. Georges sat against the other door, looking reflectively at the passing scenery.

"Has it occurred to anyone," he asked, finally, "how incredibly inept the police have been about this whole thing? You'd think that it wasn't a possible murder they were investigating but something more in the line of a petty theft."

"Oh, I don't know," said Paul. "I have to register every day at St. Etienne to make sure I don't try to leave the country."

"That's because you're not French. Here I go off on business for the next four or five days, and they've asked me to prepare an itinerary of my stops, but no check-in in the towns themselves. If I had killed Marcel, I could be beyond Algeria if I decided to leave. It makes no sense."

"It's the war," I said. "Even forgetting that the heart of

the force is gone to fight at the front, for the rest, all of their routines are upset, and without their routines . . ."

"Well, they might as well be at the front for all the good they do here."

"Now, Georges," said Paul, "I suppose they're doing something, and we just don't know about it. Besides, if you decided to go to Africa, that would be punishment enough for any crime I can think of. What heat!"

We were approaching St. Etienne, and Paul asked to be let out at a crossroads on the outskirts of town.

"I live just about a mile down the road. I mean two kilometers. And I feel like walking. I'll see you all—when?"

"Wednesday?" I ventured. "It would be good to get back to normal." Actually, it would be good to be able to predict where everyone would be at a certain time.

"I don't know if I want to be in that room for a time, though," Paul said. "Why don't we make it somewhere else next week?"

"Fine. I'll get back to you. Is that all right with you, Georges?"

He nodded.

"Okay, then," said Paul, "see you later. *Ciao.*"

With that, he turned and started up the road. Georges and I decided to light up cigarettes, and so had not yet driven off when Paul stopped two hundred meters away. A man stepped out from behind one of the trees lining the road and spoke to him. At that distance, I could see nothing descriptive. Since Georges was facing me, he saw nothing; and so without saying anything I engaged the gears and began to move. When I glanced back, both men had gone.

We continued on to St. Etienne, content to remain silent. I was wondering about Paul; in fact, by this time, I was wondering about everyone.

"Do you have time for a drink?" I asked Georges.

"Always."

We stopped at a small, dark bar, and each of us ordered a cognac. We sat near the door, watching over the car and its load.

"What's your business here?" asked Georges.

"Oh, I'm supposed to see some people about a vine graft. In fact, with all this mess about Marcel, I'm afraid I don't feel like doing any kind of business. I was wondering if I could help you in your deliveries. Tania has told me a lot about the factory, or asenal, here. Whatever it is. Her friend Maurice Ponty is the director, and I'd like to see it. Keep my mind from . . . from other things."

"Delighted, Jules! I could use the company. Maybe Ponty could show us around. Normally I only deliver to the gates."

"Oh, you've never been inside?" Somehow I was both relieved and disappointed.

"No. Tight security and all that. Normally Henri and I come down together and leave everything with the attendants."

"Hmm . . ." I said, rather pointlessly.

We finished our drinks and returned to the car. After a few more minutes of driving, we reached our destination.

The St. Etienne Arsenal and Munitions Factory was indeed a large and modern affair. It covered several hundred square meters of land on the eastern edge of the city, bounded by what must have been a tributary of the Rhone that carried away much of the waste. When the day was clear, and the wind from the right direction, you could see the smoke from the stacks as far away as Valence; a thick, sulfurous cloud usually hung over the structure. Brick chimneys to a height of nearly thirty meters had been built to lift the smoke so that it wouldn't settle on the nearby houses. The entire structure was surrounded by a fence of barbed wire and guarded every twenty-five meters or so by troops. The building itself was made of a kind of adobe, which was originally white, but even in the short time since its opening had turned a sickly, dirty yellow.

We went first to the delivery area, where Georges presented his papers and unloaded his supplies. Then we drove to the main gate, parked, and approached the sentry box.

"Yes, what do you want?" said the guard.

"We'd like to visit, if we may," Georges replied.

The guard laughed heartily. "Impossible."

Georges and I looked helplessly at one another, and he began again. "But I've been delivering here since you've opened. We'd just like to look around inside."

The guard stopped laughing and blew on his whistle. Within seconds, four other guards had run up, weapons at the ready. I decided to speak.

"I'd like to see Monsieur Ponty."

At the mention of the director's name, the guards looked at one another indecisively. Finally one of them went into the building. After about ten minutes, which seemed much longer because of the heat and the circumstances, the guard returned with a short, round, cheerful-looking man.

"You asked for me? I am Monsieur Ponty."

"Yes. I am a friend of Tania Chessal. She's spoken so much

to me about your operation here. I'd hoped to be privileged with a look for myself. Jules Giraud is my name."

There was a hint of recognition in his eyes, and he nodded to the guards, who started back to their posts.

"And this man?" he asked, indicating Georges.

"Georges Lavoie, monsieur. He has been delivering your medical supplies for some time, and is a personal friend."

He stared for another moment. "Come with me."

We crossed the wide yard of gravel, and I couldn't help noticing the scrutiny with which we were observed from every direction. There were sentries posted at the gates, along the fence, at selected bunkers in the yard, and on the roof. Ponty seemed to notice my interest, and smiled.

He led us through the large glass doors and down a long corridor to his office, the second room on the right. I was surprised to find it so well furnished. There was a bright rug covering the floor, and several prints on the walls, including Van Gogh's *The Field at Arles* which I thought a very strange choice for the director of an arsenal. To the right, behind his desk, were filing cabinets of a light, drab wood; and, to the left, an elegant bar. His desk itself was a flat and large slab of oak which rested on unfinished timbers, although the joints were perfectly matched. It was an efficient office, though not without personality.

We were seated.

"So, you are Jules Giraud. Tania speaks of you often."

I inclined my head slightly. "She's quite impressed with you and this place, you know? Have you known her long?"

"Oh, quite some time. I knew her husband before they were married. A fine man. You knew Jean?"

"Yes, he was my neighbor."

"Ah, yes, yes. Of course."

I didn't wish to speak of Jean Chessal, especially to a friend of his. My conscience was not completely clear regarding him.

"And how is Tania?" he asked.

"Quite well," I said, not entirely truthfully. "She sends her best."

He smiled. "Do ask her to come by soon. She is a welcome guest anytime. She doesn't visit nearly enough."

"I will ask her, though I somehow didn't think you solicited visitors here. The guards . . ."

We all laughed. Then, in a brusque but friendly way, he clapped his hands together and sat up straight.

"Now, what can I do for you?"

"Well, frankly, we decided to come to see you mostly out of curiosity. Monsieur Lavoie, here, had some deliveries to make, and I had other business in town, which I chose to put off. Tania had told me so much about this building, and about yourself, that I thought I'd come by to meet you and to see some of your innovations."

"You did, did you?" There was more than a bit of flint in the mildly humorous gaze.

I raised a hand. "Please stop me if I'm out of line."

"Be assured that I would, monsieur. It is no small matter that you have been allowed to come this far. You're aware of that, of course." It wasn't a question, and he continued. "But then we've carried on this farce long enough. It isn't every day that one meets such a serious rival face-to-face, is it?"

"I'm afraid I don't completely understand," I said.

"Come, come, Monsieur Giraud. Surely you don't think just anyone can enter this compound. And I do think I'm justified in calling it precisely that. Probably there isn't another man, or men"—here he motioned to Georges—"in France that I would have allowed within these walls without an official reason. 'Just wanted to look over your innovations!' Indeed!" He chuckled at my ludicrous suggestion. "I admit that bringing a visitor along with you, and one with actual business here, is a charming touch that shows real imagination, and I begin to see what Tania is talking about. But let's admit the facts, that you came by here for the same reason that I let you in—plain curiosity, all right—and not about our innovations."

Georges picked up the tenuous threads. "He's found you out, Jules, No doubt of it."

"All right," I said, forcing a grin. I had no choice but to press on, hoping that Ponty would drop some further clue as to what he was talking about. "I'll admit it—I simply had to discover what it was all about."

The director looked suitably downcast. "It's about love."

"Yes," I answered, "it is about love."

"She told you, then, about my proposal?"

"Of course," I said, my stomach sinking since in fact she'd told me no such thing. "Just the other day."

"Yes, I expected she would have. I must admit I never entertained much hope, but I had to try."

Again Georges came to my rescue. "She is a remarkable woman," he said. "Who could blame you?"

Ponty sighed deeply. Then, again clapping his hands softly in what I took to be a characteristic gesture, he regained his businesslike composure. "Well, I am glad to meet you after all. If I have to lose her, it is some comfort to meet the man and realize that he is a gentleman."

I accepted the compliment with a nod, nearly overcome with relief that Tania had turned him down, then distressed anew by the secrets she kept from me. But this was no time to reflect on that. "I'm sorry if my curiosity seems callous," I said. "I had no intention—"

"Please," he said, waving me off, "put the thought from your mind. What could be more natural? But to satisfy your curiosity about me completely, I suppose I should show you our operations here after all, eh? How does the saying go— 'judge a man by his creation'? The St. Etienne arsenal is my 'creation,' Monsieur Giraud. It is the thing of which I am most proud."

At that moment a guard passed in the hall and looked in, prompting Georges to speak up. "Frankly, I'm very impressed with your security."

"Yes," Ponty replied. "I doubt rather strongly that anything save a massive assault could cause us much inconvenience. I might add, we don't envision an assault of that kind around here. Still, considering the kind of work we're doing, we can't be too careful. Come."

We rose and went back out to the corridor. He turned to Georges.

"What is it that you deliver?"

"Medical supplies. Gauze, bandages, no real medicine."

"Ah, yes. Fortunately, we haven't had many accidents. I hope we can keep your deliveries small. Now, then"—he stopped in front of the first door we'd passed coming in—"as

you know, we make most kinds of arms and munitions supplies here, so really our security amounts to national security.
Open that door, Monsieur Giraud."

I stepped up to the heavy door and found it locked.

Ponty squatted down and slid a card under the door, then
knocked four times. The door swung open from within onto
a small, closetlike enclosure. On either side of the space sat
an armed guard. The room was devoid of decoration and
contained only a door against the opposite wall. Ponty
walked across the tiny area to that door and tried it, but it
too was locked. Then he turned and walked back to us, closing the first door behind him.

"The explosives room," he explained. "We change the
guards every three hours because the anteroom is so . . . you
saw it. With every shift, we change the card-and-knock se-
quence. I don't mind telling you this because the guards are
under orders to shoot to kill anyone who gets them to open
the doors by deception. Only myself, my immediate assis-
tant, or the guards' replacements may be admitted into that
room. Anyone else will be shot."

I said soberly, "But you had me try the door."

Ponty laughed. "A perfect way to eliminate my archrival,
yes? But you see, you were in no danger. Only if you had
had my card, knocked four times, and been admitted would
you have been shot. I'm sorry if I scared you."

I held up a hand, laughing hollowly. "I don't scare that
easily."

He waited for a moment at the door to the explosives
room. A janitor pushing a wide broom shuffled his way past
us, not so much as lifting his head to acknowledge us. Ponty

seemed to be observing him carefully. Clearly the presence of visitors would not be viewed as an excuse to slack off on duties.

"Friendly chap," I ventured.

Ponty shrugged. "Nervous, I guess. Some of 'em are, here." He sighed. "I guess it isn't the easiest thing in the world, working inside what amounts to the biggest bomb in France."

Georges cleared his throat, and Ponty took that as a signal to continue our tour. The next door down the hallway opened into an enormous cacophonous inferno, but Ponty had no hesitancy about gesturing us in. Four huge boilers hissed and steamed against one wall to our right, while two shovel-wielding stevedores fed coal to the burners under them. The room's temperature was staggering.

Like a proud homeowner, Ponty walked us around. The boilers were of heavily reinforced steel, loaded with gauges that screamed under their internal pressures. Lining the back wall of the room was a small mountain of coal being slowly chipped away by the workers. Dozens of arteries—insulated piping—emanated from the heart of the arsenal's power plant.

"What goes on here?" Georges yelled over the din.

Ponty motioned us back outside into the relative cool of the hall. He was beaming. "Impressive, isn't it?"

"Is every room here frightening?" Georges asked.

"That frightened you?"

"It's a vision of hell."

Ponty chuckled. "Well, put like that, I suppose one might say it is, after all."

"It did seem awesomely powerful."

He nodded. "It has to be. We've got power needs here

that I can't discuss, but they rival those of many small towns. In effect, we've got our own generator. We've got to be able to control our power, keep it regular, allow no surges. Am I getting too technical?"

"Not at all," Georges said.

"It's rather fascinating," I agreed.

We turned a corner and entered another long and narrow hall. Ponty's words echoed off the bare walls, mingling with the memory of the other room's straining engines. I was beginning to feel the building more as a living thing, and could understand Ponty's nearly paternal pride in its structure as well as his fear for its safety.

"You see," he said, "although much of the work we do here is production line stuff—making ammunition and so on—there is also a great deal of stress-related research and testing. To say nothing of the power needed to keep a place like this heated and lit over three shifts seven days a week. Those boilers never shut down."

Georges seemed to be pondering something. "But compared to the ammunition room, they seemed poorly guarded."

The point seemed to come home to Ponty. "You know, they may be, now that you mention it. But there is so much here that must be guarded full-time—explosives are one example; the research rooms are another—and we do only have so many men. I guess we have to draw the line somewhere."

"It seems somehow"—Georges paused, looking for the right word—"less thorough, I suppose."

Ponty stopped before a pair of double doors, which, we would soon discover, led to the development rooms for armored vehicles. But before we entered, he wanted to close the book on this discussion. It probably seemed to him as though we were calling his procedures into question, and he wanted to set the record straight.

"Monsieur Lavoie," he said, "you forget that you are taking this tour with me, the director. The men shoveling coal in that room are soldiers, as are nearly all members of the staff. Perhaps you didn't notice the weapons on their belts?"

Georges shook his head.

"Ah, just so. Anyone entering any room here without authorization does so at tremendous risk to his own life, I assure you."

"And there are always soldiers there?"

"We can never let our power go down. I will tell you frankly, though I can't be too specific, that certain researches we are undertaking, certain chemicals and so on, are held in an extremely precarious balance by electrical currents and constant temperatures, among other things. Slight fluctuations can be fatal. No, we take extreme care."

"I'm sure Georges didn't mean to imply any negligence." I tried to calm our host.

"Certainly not," Georges replied. "I was merely curious."

But Ponty had one more nail to hammer home. "All our rooms are manned at all times. Even my own office, now sitting empty, is guarded. We don't let up our vigilance, ever!"

I was glad I was with Georges, with his cosmopolitan air. He smiled suavely, including us all into his fraternity. "And we are most grateful for that vigilance, sir. The whole country is grateful."

Ponty took obvious satisfaction in the compliment. His

eyes darted quickly to me and I nodded, hoping my unspo-
ken affirmation would lessen the sense of rivalry.

Georges continued. "The whole thing is just so amazing
to me. I've come here so often to deliver, and I've seen your
men loading for large deliveries. The logistics are just too
awesome to comprehend. It seems as though every man in
France is out there helping load munitions for the front."

Ponty's eyes twinkled. He was obviously somewhat taken
with Georges. Often in my career and in my life, I'd noticed
that once a person has tapped one emotion in another, a
door may be opened to other emotions. Georges had angered Ponty, and the director's response had compromised
his natural reserve and professional manner. Once Georges
had cooled his anger, the door was open to friendship. We
were all, suddenly, members of the same club—men of similar natures caught up in the most serious of endeavors, un-
able to trust or love or find release from the unbearable
tensions of the times.

Ponty smiled warmly now. "I'll let you both in on something, then, since you've been so astute. When we have heavy
shipments, everyone helps, even myself. For fifteen, perhaps
twenty minutes, we are all pack mules. Except, of course,
for the guards at the explosives rooms. They never, ever leave
their posts."

Georges returned Ponty's smile. "Your secret is safe with
us, eh, Jules?"

"To our graves," I responded.

"And now," Ponty said, opening the double doors, "let
me show you . . ."

Our tour continued for the next hour or so. None of the

other rooms, it turned out, was as closely guarded as the explosives room, though security everywhere was tight.

The factory made everything from bullets and bombs to rifles and cannons. The next cavernous room was dedicated to working out the rough edges of a motorized armored car with mounted cannons, which Ponty thought would become a powerful new battlefield weapon. The preliminary sketches and models we saw were impressive, but it seemed to me that they still had a long way to go. Ponty hoped to complete a working model within six months, though, and Georges, after careful consideration, pronounced himself in agreement with that verdict. There were many other research rooms which Ponty could not show us. He apologized for this, and we both assured him we understood completely and had very much enjoyed the look around. Finally Maurice— he was "Maurice" by then—showed us to the door and bade us adieu.

"We don't have visitors very often," he said, "and, as you said, we don't want them, but it's been a pleasure showing you both around." Maurice turned to me. "Jules, I'm glad that you decided to satisfy your curiosity." With that, we shook hands and he disappeared back into the building.

Walking back to the car, Georges and I were thoughtful. It was now dusk. The factories would be closing within the hour, and I wanted to get back home.

"Life is sure full of surprises," Georges remarked, elbowing me slightly.

I said nothing but thought instead of the questions I would have for Tania.

"Very impressive place," Georges said, diplomatically changing the subject. "I wouldn't be too worried about a breach of security if I were Maurice. That anteroom scared me to death, to say nothing of the boilers."

"Yes," I said. "Unless the Germans take St. Etienne—in which case we'll have lost the war anyway—I'd say that factory is safe. Awfully modern building, isn't it?"

"I loved it. I could have stayed all day."

Something was bothering me, so I thought I'd better say it. "Yes, I noticed how acute your interest was. I thought you'd be bored in there, though I was glad you accompanied me."

"Bored? Not at all. Fascinated, truly fascinated. Perhaps I've never mentioned it, Jules, but my initial love was architecture. I studied it for years in school, and only my father's passionate belief that all art was somewhat effete—backed by his promise to withhold any financial aid to myself—persuaded me to enter the dynamic and exciting world of business." He seemed genuinely bitter, the sarcasm heavy.

"I didn't mean . . ." I began, sorry that I had touched a nerve.

"No. That's all right. People, in the end, do what they truly want to do, I suppose."

We talked on for a few more minutes before I dropped him off at a hotel. As usual, in spite of the large delivery today, he had calls to make for the remainder of the week, the weekend notwithstanding.

"Unfortunately, the need for my products keeps increasing. It may be good for business, but I find it difficult to rejoice in the fact."

"Will you be able to make it by next Wednesday?" I
asked.

"I assume so. I'll leave a message if I'm delayed."

"Fine. Until then."

The drive home was long and uneventful. I usually don't
like to drive at night, and by the time I had reached the road
to Valence, it was completely dark. My headlights flushed a
few animals along the way, but otherwise I saw nothing and
heard only the sound of the engine, which drowned out my
soft humming of the "Marseillaise."

· 7 ·

After dinner—a simple coq au vin and a bottle of beaujolais—Tania and I sat in the kitchen with brandy. The living room still made us nervous, and Fritz said he didn't mind the intrusion. So we sat on wooden chairs across the table from one another. It was a quiet night. The large stone fireplace crackled from time to time, and Fritz, cleaning up, moved easily about. When he'd finished, he turned down the lamps and left us alone. The room was a montage of pale yellow light and black shadows. Something, probably a mouse, scampered across the floor.

Tania was wearing a light blouse with a tan wraparound skirt that came to a few inches above her ankles. She was beautiful enough to get away with that kind of dress, though it would properly be considered fairly risqué. Her long hair fell across her face, and looking across at her I found it very hard to believe that she was beginning her fifth decade. I got up, came around the table, and kissed her.

"Are you feeling better?" I asked.

"Yes."

"I went to see your friend Ponty today."

Her shoulders stiffened a little. "What were you doing at the arms factory?"

"Georges had to deliver there, and I decided it would be a nice break to put off my appointment today and see this place you've talked about so much. It is a very impressive sight, though I wish they could do something about the smoke."

"I know," she said. "Isn't the smell terrible?"

"Horrible. But I suppose when one works with sulfur, that's impossible to avoid."

We heard Fritz moving about behind us in his room. He usually did exercises and then read a bit before going to bed.

"How did you find Maurice?" she asked.

I described our tour, including the little episode at the door to the explosives room. Tania smiled and said that sounded just like Maurice. We sipped at our brandy, and the silence came back to surround us. There would never be a better time.

"Tania," I began, then stopped, terrified. To me she was the most attractive woman in the world, and if I pressed on now I ran the risk of losing her. But I really had no choice—if I couldn't ask, I had already lost her. "Why didn't you tell me about Ponty's proposal?"

Her shoulders sagged slightly as she put her snifter down. "Oh," she said, "he told you about that?"

"It quite hurt me," I said truthfully.

"Oh, Jules, I'm sorry." She reached out across the table and covered my hand. "Maurice and I are only friends."

"Obviously Maurice doesn't feel the same way."

"I know. I was very surprised."

"I don't understand why you wouldn't have told me."

She shrugged, squeezing my hand. "It didn't matter. It had no effect on us. Why did you need to know?"

"Are we operating on a 'need to know' basis now?"

"What does that mean? Of course not. I just didn't think it was so important, or appropriate. And really, Jules, it isn't."

"A marriage proposal isn't important?"

"Not unless I'd have said yes, which I did not."

I covered her hand with my own and stared into her guileless and beautiful face. "I'm afraid I'm uncomfortable with these secrets between us."

She lowered her gaze and her voice. Her words seemed to have been wrung from her against her will, as though the necessity of having to admit it belied its own truth. "There are no secrets between us."

Before I could respond, there was a crashing sound against the front door. I bolted up and ran to see what it had been. Outside, the night was inky black, and I could barely make out even the shadows of trees. Faintly, though, I heard what I took to be several pairs of retreating feet and some high-pitched giggling.

Tania had brought up a lantern and stood behind me. On the ground I could make out a large rock, which I bent over to pick up. There was a paper tied to it, and on the paper a crude drawing of a skull. I turned around and found Tania crying.

"Now, now," I said, "it was simply a group of kids. You

know they do this kind of thing often enough. And especially after word spread about Marcel's murder in this house.
If you listen you can still hear them giggling. Listen."

And over the quiet fields did come the sound of young
voices, muffled and diminishing but still audible.

We moved back inside and stood in the foyer. In spite of
my words to Tania, I was shaken. This sort of thing did happen, I suppose, on occasion, but with suspicions already so
high, it did my nerves no good. I walked back to the kitchen
for another brandy, which I drank much too quickly. Coming back through the dark sitting room, I turned into the
stairway and stood transfixed by what I saw.

Tania stood silhouetted against the top of the stairs, holding the lantern in her left hand. Her recent tears still glis-
tened on her face, her hair hung to her shoulders, and she
had undone her blouse, which now hung open before her.
Very quietly she spoke: "Jules, come to bed. I'm afraid."

■ ■ ■

Later, I could not sleep. Overcome by the events of the day,
ashamed that I had doubted Tania, unnerved by the children's prank, I got up and looked out the window. The only
sound was the gurgle of the brook as it flowed through the
arbor. A crescent moon had just risen, and it was somehow
reassuring. In my mind I went over the details of the St. Etienne arsenal so that I could report the next morning to
Lupa. At my desk, I lit the lamp and sketched from memory
the general floor plan. That took my mind off my wor-
ries, and by the time I finished, I felt sleepy. I remembered,
though, to write Fritz a note to have him wake me early;

then I came back to the bed, where Tania lay, and crawled in beside her.

But just before I dozed off, I thought I heard the sound of a car engine starting, accompanied by indistinguishable voices drifting over the fields, finally fading into the noise of the engine as it roared toward St. Etienne.

· 8 ·

Tania did not stir when Fritz knocked once discreetly. I rose immediately, tapping once on my bedstead to let him know I was awake. After a fast cup of coffee and several minutes of Fritz's remonstrance over my sagging appetite, I was on my way to Lupa's.

La Couronne hadn't yet opened, but Charles stood behind the bar, dusting, and let me in after only a short wait. Lupa had given instructions that no one was to come to the kitchen without his approval, so I sat at the bar and had another coffee while Charles went to announce me.

He returned and I followed him down the narrow staircase to the kitchen. Lupa sat majestically at the table, clad in a brown silk robe with a yellow monogram, cleaning up the remainder of what had been his breakfast.

"One of the problems with being one's own cook," he began immediately, motioning me to be seated, "is deciding an order of courses that provides variety yet leaves oneself free to enjoy each course without having to tend to the next. These muffins, Jules, have become too cold while waiting for the eggs to set."

I noticed he was having no trouble, however, in finishing off the cooled muffins. The eggs had, by the looks of the plate, long since disappeared. I mentioned this to him.

"Yes, but it's not as enjoyable as it should be, as every meal should be. Every man's life is divided up into eating, sleeping, and miscellaneous. *Omnia vita in tres partes divisa est,* if I might borrow from Caesar. Of their conscious moments, only in their enjoyment of food are all men brothers."

I could think of several other conscious moments that might qualify as universally pleasing, but he was enjoying himself, so I let him expound.

"And here I am, presuming to call myself a cook, a chef. Ha! Jules, I nearly let the coffee boil!"

I shook my head sadly in commiseration. In spite of his petulance, which Tania had found so objectionable, I found him entertaining. He knew as well as anyone, possibly better than anyone, the gravity of our situation, but he wouldn't let himself be bogged down in depression. He was a tonic to my flagging spirits.

"Did you get the beer?" I asked.

"Ah, yes. Thank you. Consistently excellent. Fritz brought it around yesterday."

He pushed back his chair and settled himself more comfortably. After offering me breakfast or coffee, which I declined, he picked up his cup and sipped.

"Madame Chessal came by to see me yesterday."

"Yes, I know. She told me about it."

"She seemed rather upset by my lack of interest in the, ahem, proprieties. I tried to explain to her that worry merely clouds the intellect, that I meant no slight to Monsieur Routier, that I had been enthusiastic about sausage because I was talking about sausage, and that enthusiasm is a state of mind I try to cultivate about many subjects. I'm afraid my explanation fell on deaf ears. She left in rather a huff."

"She was upset about Marcel," I said. "They'd known each other a long time."

"I understand that. But you understand I didn't want to discuss Marcel's death with her until I was certain she was not involved."

"Are you?" I asked hopefully.

"Unfortunately, no."

"You're serious, aren't you?"

"Perfectly, Jules, perfectly."

How could I allay his suspicions when only yesterday I had harbored them myself? Still, I forced a response. "At the risk of usurping your methods, do you have anything specific, or is it just a feeling?"

Lupa sipped again at his coffee, smacked his lips with pleasure, then looked levelly at me across his desk. "The questions I have regarding Madame Chessal's involvement in our inquiries fall into both categories. First, I must confess to a certain feeling that in a general way she is not being completely forthright, that she is hiding something. It may be nothing. It may be that she cultivates an aura of mystery. Many women do, you know, believing that it makes them interesting. In fact, it creates an impression of a fascinating personality that is all the more disappointing when the aura itself is revealed to be a sham." He continued before I could remonstrate. "I don't say that is the case here. I merely comment on my feeling.

"Specifically, there are several points. My operatives have stumbled on Madame Chessal many times in and around St. Etienne. She certainly has ready access to the arsenal there. As you yourself have pointed out, she has a relationship of some sort with the director. Secondly, poison is a classic woman's weapon for murder. Additionally, I find it worthy of note that she is the only woman in what would otherwise be a vigorously masculine grouping."

"How is that noteworthy?" I had to cut in. His suspicions of Tania seemed to me to be no more than a general indictment of female human beings, and I told him so.

"It's true. I do have a prejudice there, probably inherited from my father. But I have verified it on my own many times."

"But we're talking specifically here about Tania."

"I understand that. Don't become upset, Jules. I would expect you to defend her, to be blind to the striking singularity of one woman fitting in so easily with five or six different men. It is certainly odd enough to be labeled a hard fact and to warrant some explanation."

"She has always . . ."

"Not true! I understand that she only began attending regularly within the past year or two."

"With her husband in the area, how could she?"

He smiled, his point won, and finished his coffee in a gulp. "I merely state that it is worthy of investigation, and I intend to look into it. There are other issues that I would prefer for the time being to keep to myself, but I assure you that I view them as significant, or potentially significant. But come. This is a small avenue of pursuit, and we have much more to discuss. Shall we table Madame Chessal for the moment?"

Reluctantly, but seeing the wisdom of the suggestion, I agreed and told him I had the plans for the arsenal with me. He asked me to wait until he'd dressed and then I could report at length. Excusing himself, he went into his quarters.

Almost immediately I heard two voices coming from his rooms. One his, the other female. The woman sounded angry and became more so as they talked. Finally, after several minutes of increasing volume, came the sound of a hand slapping down violently on a table or desk, and Lupa's voice, not loud, but devastatingly authoritative: "Enough! Leave! We'll discuss this later." Then he appeared back in the kitchen.

"Bah," he said, sitting down, "I'm sorry about that, but that woman nags me much too often. Do all women insist on scheduling time for their men?"

"Not to my knowledge," I said.

"Well, I won't have it." He leaned back and closed his eyes for a moment, his face clearing almost instantly. He had excellent control. "Now, then, those plans."

I took the crumpled and hastily drawn sketch from my pocket, and together we looked at it. I explained some of my impressions of the place, pointing out that the arsenal was impossible to enter forcibly. In my years as an agent, I've learned to recall almost completely events, conversations, and impressions, which was lucky, since he asked me to recount everything that had happened the day before since I'd met Tania for the funeral. He leaned back with his eyes nearly closed, and didn't move at all as I talked.

He interrupted me three times. Once to ask if I could identify the man I'd seen meet Paul. Once to ask me to repeat everything I could remember Ponty saying from the time we met him until we were shown the explosives anteroom, and again to ask if I was certain that the rock-throwing incident had been a prank, to which I answered no, I wasn't certain of anything.

When I'd finished, he said, "Pulis?"

"As far as I know, he spent the day consoling his wife."

"He also spent the better part of the afternoon reading a newspaper at the train station," he said. "Can you think of why he might have done that?"

I shook my head no.

"You should call on him, I suppose. You haven't aroused suspicion with any of them, have you?"

"No. I've decided to have another beer gathering next Wednesday, though I'm not sure where it ought to be. That will give everyone a chance to get back together, restore our confidence in one another, lay some suspicion to rest. Most of them seem to want to believe it was suicide."

"Rubbish!"

"I know, but let them think that for a time. It won't make them wary of me when I ask questions, or at least less wary than if they thought I suspected one of them had killed him."

"Satisfactory," was all he said. I asked him if he'd had any trouble with the police.

"No."

"They haven't been around?" I asked.

"I didn't say that. I merely said I haven't had any trouble with them. I wouldn't speak with them. Charles told them I had gone shopping and I would call them back at my convenience. Then they wanted to search my quarters, which of course would have been intolerable, so Charles said he didn't know where I lived, and they believed him. One thing I don't need at a time like this is the police. I assume they're content to believe it was suicide also?"

I shrugged, since I really didn't know.

"All right," he said. "I'll try to avoid being bothered by them, though when they find out I live here, they'll be around snooping for cyanide and whatnot."

"They haven't been much of a bother to me," I said. I found the police no more competent than he did, but I saw no reason to antagonize them gratuitously.

"You are a rich man, Jules. You have standing in this area. You are, in short, more or less above suspicion. I am poor, a foreigner, unknown—in short, a perfect scapegoat. Of course I could demonstrate my innocence if given enough time, or I could save that time by delivering the murderer. And time is short."

So saying, he took a large silver watch from his vest pocket. All the times I had seen him, he'd been wearing suits of drab brown. He never looked seedy, but neither would well-dressed be an adequate description. Today was no exception, though he had slipped a vest over the pale yellow shirt. He wore no coat while indoors, and when he cooked he wore no tie. Glancing at his watch, he started.

"Nearly nine o'clock! I must be up on the street." He was peeved, I supposed at me for coming down and causing him to vary his schedule. When we'd gotten settled outside, I commented on the watch, which I hadn't seen before.

"Yes, it is lovely," he said, removing it again. "A gift from my parents, one of my few real treasures. Would you like to see it?"

He handed it across to me. It was rather larger than was the fashion and seemed to be made of very pure silver, judging from the weight. Turning it over in my hands, I noticed the inscription on the back, or rather the pair of initials, s. h. & i. a. and the date 1897. I was curious, but said nothing and gave it back to him.

"One of my fondest dreams is to someday own a house where I can keep things," he began. "Traveling has so long uprooted me that I think someday I would like a home where I could keep the things I love. I could easily envision myself almost totally sedentary. But now this watch is the only symbol I have of all I would like to have." He sighed.

"I'm surprised to find you so materialistic."

"Not at all. I want nothing more than what the simplest shopkeeper has: a house, a sense of place, a few loved possessions. So often a man's surroundings become a man's background. A man who runs with thieves becomes like a thief. Of course," he went on, stopping to order the first of his day's beers, "it's not absolute, but I'd like a house made for my ideals, so that I might grow into it."

He paused while the beer—my beer!—arrived. Charles had thoughtfully brought out two bottles, and we each had a glass.

"Take yourself, Jules. You are an aristocrat. No, no, don't object—that's not so bad. You own land, a house. Your interests are your own, not dictated by the exigencies of survival. And it shows. The other night, even drunk, you paused to wipe off a table before setting anything on it, even when it was a patently futile gesture. No, the way you live reinforces the way you act; the way you act finally becomes the way you are."

By this time, I was anxious to be off to visit Henri. I had probably been much like Lupa when I'd been younger. He was so enthusiastic about ideas, about ideals. I couldn't remember ever having known anyone so opinionated, but he wasn't so much objectionable or obnoxious as time-consuming, and as he'd said, time was short. I finished my beer and rose to leave as Charles brought out another one for Lupa, along with a clutch of newspapers. He looked up briefly.

"Will I see you?"

I had barely nodded when he looked back down, engrossed in his reading.

■ ■ ■

Henri lived in a large apartment overlooking his shop. It was a good distance from La Couronne, so I decided to take a hansom and enjoy the warm morning. I remember not being overly concerned with whether taking a hansom was a particularly aristocratic thing to do or not. It was a pleasant ride over the cobbled streets, and in a quarter of an hour I found myself in front of Henri's door. His eldest son was minding the shop, which was not surprising. I was a regular customer because of my beer supplies, and the sons knew me slightly. Some flaw in my character keeps me from remembering the names of children, and this boy was no exception. So I entered the small and cluttered store and approached the gangling youth with a warm smile of recognition.

"Bonjour, Monsieur Giraud."

Likewise, it seems to me that all children remember my name and glory in greeting me this way.

We shook hands.

"Good morning. Is your father here?"

"He's above."

"Thank you."

Smiling to myself, I walked over to the door that opened onto the staircase and knocked. The boy had followed me over and he turned the knob for me.

"That's all right. Go on up."

Henri sat at the kitchen table, leaning back in his blue work pants and apron. None of the other children were about, though noises behind me suggested their presence somewhere in the flat. Madame Pulis was cutting onions and putting them in a large skillet over the fire. I stood in the archway for a moment looking at the scene before knocking on the doorjamb.

They both turned at once. Madame Pulis's eyes were filled with tears, I assumed from the onions. Henri, seeing me, immediately jumped up and put out his hand in greeting. He seemed even more nervous than usual.

As we sat at the table, we watched his wife finish cutting the onions, and then he ordered her from the room. My Greek friend, now slumping slightly over the table, hands clasped tightly in front of him, was a study in anxiety. His hair was disheveled, as though it had been combed earlier but something, perhaps nervous hands, had disturbed it. There was an unfamiliar tic over his right eye, which further enhanced his harried mien. He looked a wreck.

When his wife had gone, he looked at me heavily.

"What's wrong, Henri? You look terrible."

He got up abruptly and paced back and forth slowly across the kitchen, pulling—jerking, really—all the while at his mustache. "It all started yesterday with Renee. You remember? At the funeral? She was crying a lot? Well, it really got to her, all the folks there were treating us as if we were guilty of something, and so she was crying. She cries easily." He stopped walking and looked at me imploringly.

"All that was fine. If you know Renee, you'd know crying is no special event. But some plainclothes *flic* at the funeral thought it was strange that one of the 'suspect's' wives should even bother coming, much less be in tears, so he thought we might know something and followed us home." He sat down again. "You know me, Jules. I get nervous easily and, when he came around, I got rattled. And with Renee crying all over, I just walked out. I know, I know, a mistake. I snuck out, really. I'm a fool.

"So then he started in on Renee. What were my feelings about Marcel? How well had she known him? You know how insinuating they can be, and he was, but she'd only met Marcel maybe twice, so what could she say? Finally, he asks if he can look around the house, and she says we have nothing to hide, so he goes poking into everything and finds the supplies for Robert—you know my second son? Anyway, he finds Robert's supplies for taking photographs, which is his hobby, and right there in a drawer is plenty of cyanide to kill

Marcel and a hundred other people, so he says, 'Uh-huh, interesting,' and leaves. So when I got home at about six o'clock, there's no dinner and the house is dark, and she's left a note that says she's gone to stay with her mother and taken the kids, and I can come get her later.

"Not wanting to wait for her to come back, I decided to go over there and find out what happened, and who do I run into on the street but this same *flic*, come to ask Renee some more questions. He looks at me for a minute and then says, 'You're not a French citizen, are you?' "

He paused for a moment. "I'd like a drink." He rose and got two glasses, filling one nearly to the top with pastis. In the other glass, he put a standard shot and added water. He grinned nervously, handing me the second glass. "Straight, it's just like ouzo. Makes me feel at home." He pulled again and again at his mustache, taking slow little sips of the drink. Every few seconds, he scratched at his head. "*Merde!* Where was I?"

"Are you a French citizen?"

"That's right, French citizen. Well, I told him that my papers were in order, that he could see for himself if he came back to the house, but he just started asking more questions about everybody. You, Georges, Paul, even Tania. Wanted to know if I knew where that fellow Lupa lived. I told him I didn't know anything, I didn't know Lupa, I hardly had known Marcel. Then he started going on again about how well had Renee and Marcel known each other, and it got fairly heated. He said he was going to check all the other houses—Tania's, yours, Paul's—and then get back to me, so I'd better find my wife and be available."

"What did you do after that?"

He was loosening up, as he always did when he drank. "Well, I went to get Renee. Then we all came home and tried to sleep. Goddamn it, Jules, can't a woman even cry at a funeral?"

He put his hand down, looking on the verge of tears. I put my hand lightly on his shoulder.

"Take it easy, Henri. It's just the way of investigators. They bother you, they try to find breaks in stories. Don't worry."

But I was worried. Cyanide was not so common a poison that anyone else would likely have it.

"Where did you go yesterday afternoon," I asked, "when you went wandering around?"

"Oh, I don't know. Just around. You know, when I'm upset, I walk." As if to prove his point, he got up and started pacing again. I didn't want to press it, so I changed the subject.

"I'd like to have everybody meet again next Wednesday. That's the real reason I had for coming up. Do you think you can make it?"

"I don't know," he said simply. "At your house?"

"Probably not. I'll send you a note. I thought it would be good for us all to try and . . . well, you know."

He nodded. "Will Lupa be there?"

"Yes. Do you suspect him?"

"I'd be lying if I said I didn't. How well did he know Marcel?"

I laughed. "You thinking of joining the police force?"

He smiled weakly. "You're right," he said. "I'm sorry, but

it's just that you get to suspecting everyone. But how well do you know him?"

"Fairly well."

"All right. Renee!" he yelled suddenly. "The onions are burning."

His wife came back into the room, apologetic. It was the first time I'd seen her without tears in her eyes. She was attractive in a tough sort of way—the kind of woman I'd expect Henri to be with—short, dark, buxom, subservient. She stood silently by the stove, stirring with a practiced rhythm.

"It might do you good to go down to the store," I suggested. "Take your mind off things."

I hadn't touched my drink. I offered it to him. He drank it off in a gulp.

"Let's go," he said.

On the staircase, we stopped again.

"If it's any consolation," I said, "no one came by to see either Tania or myself last night. Maybe you'll have no more trouble with him."

That seemed to make him nervous all over again. "He said he'd be back here this morning."

"Well, morning's nearly gone," I said. "What time did you run into him last night?"

"Early. Seven or half past."

"What time did you get back with your wife?"

"A few hours after that," he said. "I walked around for a while, just thinking."

We entered the shop and he called out immediately to his

son. "Henri, get those crates in line! And hang that new gar-
lic!" He turned quickly to me. "Good-bye, Jules, and thank
you. I'll let you know about next week." Then another customer entered, and Henri brushed his hands against his apron
and greeted him, as though he didn't have a worry in the
world.

Outside, it was bright and warm. Henri lived off the main
route, so I had to walk a while to get to a thoroughfare where
I could catch a hansom back to my house. I'd found his place
stuffy with the smell of grease and onions, and the walking
made me decide to stop for a beer. A boy went by with some
late editions of the newspaper, and waiting for my beer to
arrive, I idly read the news from the front. I leaned back and
relaxed, reminding myself that Henri's eldest son shared his
name, and wondering if Henri would be persuaded to come
next Wednesday. But where, it seemed, was a problem. Maybe
Lupa would have a suggestion.

I turned the pages of the *journal*, coming eventually to local news. Then I froze, my beer halfway to my mouth. I put
the beer down and looked at the small heading at the bottom
of the page. The article read:

INVESTIGATOR KILLED

Police this morning discovered the body of special investigator J. Chatelet, 46, near the outskirts of Valence. The
body lay just off the road, partially concealed in a clump
of bushes. Chatelet had been with the police for ten
years, the past five as an undercover (plainclothes) investigator. He appeared to have been strangled last night after
having been attacked from behind. The body was still

armed. He had been investigating the recent murder of Marcel Routier, a Valence salesman. He is survived by his wife, Paulette, and their three children.

I put down the paper and stared across the street, which shimmered in the heat. Folding the newspaper carefully, I put it under my arm, left some coins on the table and, standing up, flagged a carriage.

· 9 ·

"Of course I've read it," Lupa said. "I saw it only a few minutes after you left. Naturally it's interesting that he'd just been to see Pulis, but it proves nothing."

I'd gone back to Lupa's after I'd collected my thoughts. He was not at his table on the street, so I passed down under Charles's gaze to the kitchen and on back. He was not in his apartments either, so I walked into the office, took a candle, and entered the tunnel. At the other end, the lights were on and especially brilliant after the darkness.

Lupa was leaning over, staring intently at some blooming flowers, seemingly lost to any intrigue that might be encircling him. We greeted each other, and then he said something about the peace of working with flora. I had no reply. Rather, I asked him if he'd read about Chatelet's death.

"One thing it proves is that Tania is out of it," I said.

He stopped fooling with the plants and straightened up, sighing. "My dear Jules, I realize how much of a burden this must be for you to bear, but it proves nothing of the sort. Didn't you tell me you got home long after dark last night?"

"Yes."

"It became dark some time after seven last night. The sun set at six fifty-two. The ride from St. Etienne takes over an hour, and it was dark when you left, meaning that it must have been after eight when you got to Madame Chessal's home. Chatelet left Pulis at around seven. Unfortunately, that left ample time for Madame Chessal to go do nearly any mischief she had to. I admit it isn't the most likely explanation, but it is possible."

"But the man was strangled."

"Yes, that's the official explanation, pending an autopsy. Even so, one shouldn't underestimate the strength of women. It's true that they often appear helpless and weak, but that's often our perception either because that's what we expect to see, or because that's what they allow us to see. I read recently where a mother lifted a carriage that had driven over the legs of her son, a carriage I'm sure neither you nor I could have lifted. Nor at any other time might she have been able to lift it, for that matter. Stress does strange things to people, as it's doing now to you. Sit down, would you?"

I complied.

"You're overwrought. Collect yourself or you'll be worthless to both of us. Now, look around you. Breathe deeply. There is always beauty and it is always a comfort."

He was right. In a few moments, I felt calm and competent to think again. In the meantime, he didn't bother me but kept busy with the plants. Finally, he walked back to me.

"Well," he asked, "is it Pulis?"

I told him what I thought—that I wasn't sure, that my biggest problem was motive. Henri couldn't very well have been a spy for several years, since he'd been here in Valence with his growing family and business. Lupa seemed to agree, though he said nothing. When I finished reporting, he suggested I walk through the plant room with him before returning through the tunnel.

"You know that cyanide is also used to smelt gold or silver from ore. It's such a convenient poison because it's so easily attainable legally. Any photographer would have it, as would any geologist." He shrugged. "No, come to think of it, I don't believe I'll go in to see Anna today. I'll let her stew a bit over this morning's display. Come, there's work to do."

We went together back to the tunnel. I noticed him reach up just inside the door of the plant room and throw a switch.

"We can go back through now. I've turned off the alarm." I hadn't noticed that switch in my earlier passages—another indication of my decreasing powers.

Back in his office, he sat behind his desk after getting out three bottles of beer, two for himself and one for me.

After a great gulp of beer, he spoke. "I've decided it might be wise to have everyone meet here next Wednesday. Naturally, they'll be brooding about recent events, and they may resent me, but I think we can come up with something to make this place acceptable. What do you say?"

"I'm not sure," I answered truthfully. "Some of them may not come."

"If we can think of some way to get them all here, what would you say?"

"I wouldn't have any objections, I suppose. Why here, though?"

"Staging. If I can get them all in one place and question them, I think we may get somewhere. It may be easier to heighten the atmosphere of distrust here than elsewhere, and animosity is a much better catalyst than cooperation."

I drank my beer. "All right. I'll think about a way to arrange it."

"One other thing," he said.

"What's that?"

"I'd be curious to see a photograph of Madame Chessal's family. Could you get your hands on one?"

"Are you serious?"

"Perfectly."

"But why?"

"Because, Jules, I would like to lay to rest, once and for all, my suspicion of her, and I have an idea."

"You have an idea . . ." I said skeptically.

"Please," he said, "if it's a difficult request, I retract it." He seemed genuinely concerned for me. "I don't want to upset you."

"That's all right," I said. "I'm being peevish. I'll see what I can do."

"Thank you," he said simply. "It might be important."

■ ■ ■

That night I was alone at my house. Saturday was Fritz's night off, and Tania had left, I imagine, sometime during the day. I was somewhat surprised by Fritz's absence—normally he stayed at the house even on Saturdays—but of course he was perfectly free to go out. Perhaps he'd met a girl while shopping, though he was very shy with women and seemed not to like them particularly. It had taken him some months to be natural with Tania, who was the mildest of creatures.

Beset with a certain heaviness, I wandered about the large and empty house. I felt I should know more, that enough had happened to form some conclusions, but the problem was that—much as I hated to admit it—the actions of everyone involved invited suspicion. I lit a cigarette and sat on the darkened stairs. The house itself had an eeriness clinging to it. Something was making me nervous, possibly a sagging belief in my own competence. I felt I should file a report to Paris, but somehow, even with Marcel's death, there seemed nothing to report. It all seemed so parochial now, a personal matter having nothing to do with the war or with France. I felt out of touch with any national effort, and trapped in a tightening circle of local intrigue.

After a small supper of reheated stuffed bell peppers, endive salad, and several glasses of beaujolais, I tried to read, but found I couldn't shake this feeling of unease. I checked the doors to see that they were locked and then, turning off all the lights save one, went upstairs to my room for the first time since I'd left it that morning.

I had nearly finished undressing before I noticed something on my desk. I crossed over to it, sat down, lit another cigarette. It was a familiar bit of folded paper, probably left for Fritz earlier in the day with instructions to deliver it to me. Opening it, I saw several columns listing farm produce with asking prices in various locations. Wearily, I pulled the tattered code book from where I had it taped under my desk. Smoke from my cigarette burned in my eyes, and I stubbed

out the butt on the desk top, impatiently brushing the ashes
to the floor. In a few minutes I had the message entirely
decoded.

Paris had taken the initiative. They were transferring me
to Bordeaux, again for what I interpreted to be desk work,
since there was no active theater there. I went downstairs and
poured myself a cognac. I'd been moved many times in my
career, but I'd never been dismissed from a case before it had
been solved. Apparently Paris had decided that I was useless
here, or that my usefulness in general was at an end. I paced.

Finally I sat down and pulled my pad in front of me, beginning the even more complicated process of composing a
detailed response in code. I would not go to Bordeaux, even
if it meant resigning. With that thought, I sat bolt upright
and crossed out what I had begun to write. Sometimes a
course of action seems impossible until it is defined; once
defined, it becomes inevitable. I leaned back in my chair and
heaved a huge sigh of relief.

The carefully worded response was completed just as I
heard the lock turn in the front door. I came to the head of
the stairs and saw Fritz enter. He took off his coat and hung
it neatly on a peg in the hall. I called out his name.

He looked up. "Sir?"

"Pleasant evening?"

"Yes."

"Would you care for a cognac?"

"I believe I would, thank you."

I came down and we went into the sitting room. He naturally refilled my glass, then poured his own drink. I handed

him the note I'd written and asked him to mail it for me the next day.

"Certainly." He paused, sipping at his drink. "Madame Chessal took me to dinner this evening. Perhaps it's none of my affair, sir, but she seemed quite worried about you. She said to remind you that you were picnicking tomorrow. I've already planned a lunch," he added.

"Yes. I remember. What did she say?"

"Only that she was afraid you were in some special danger. I assume relating to Monsieur Routier's death. I confess that I've been concerned about your appetite recently. Did you read that one of the men investigating his death was killed last night?"

"Yes."

"Well, madame seems to think there is a kind of plot, and that you're somehow deeply involved."

I shook my head slowly. "Well, you know women, Fritz. They worry about little things. I'm not sure that Marcel's death was not suicide, and that investigator may simply have been robbed. I assure you I'm in no plot. Marcel's death did upset me, and business has been weighing me down— unnecessarily, I think— for several weeks. In fact, that note you are holding is a letter of resignation. I've decided to stay here in Valence and live out my days in what peace I can hold on to. God knows I don't need the money, and I do need a rest."

He nodded. "I think that's a good idea, sir."

"Well, fine," I said. "I think I'll be going to bed now. Would you again wake me early?" I raised my glass. "To victory, France, and peace."

We drank the toast and retired.

· 10 ·

The next morning, I picked up Tania at nine o'clock, and we took her carriage into town for Mass. It was a grand morning, and when I told Tania of my plans to stay in Valence, she threw her arms around me and laughed like a schoolgirl.

"Jules, that's wonderful!"

We sat happily through the service, and I resolved to forget my business for at least a day. Though I had resigned, I had no intention of giving up the investigation of Marcel's death. It was a matter both of pride and survival, for I entertained no doubts that all of us were indeed in some special danger.

I wondered whether Paris would respect my reply or whether they would be difficult. I had worked for them for over thirty years and undeniably knew many secrets, codes, and strategies. The situation might become very sticky. They could be most persuasive if they had to be. I put the thought out of my mind. I would have to deal with that later. For the time being, Lupa might not have been convinced of Tania's innocence, but I was. It was a good feeling.

We returned to my home and picked up the basket lunch Fritz had prepared: a cold roast chicken, hard-boiled eggs, several bottles of beer, and some dried fruits. He'd even managed to find a bit of brick chocolate for dessert.

We left the house and followed the brook across the road and down into the meadow beyond, where a few field horses grazed peacefully. I carried the small folding table and chairs, and Tania the basket. About two kilometers downstream, the brook widens into a placid pond, dotted here and there with fowl and surrounded by a rather dense woods. We picked our way into one of the several clearings and set up the table, which Tania covered with the plain white cloth Fritz had given us. Then she took off her bonnet and shoes and went to wade in the pond. I sat and watched her, absentmindedly shelling an egg.

I called to her, and she came back to the table. We drank beer and ate slowly, talking of food and books. She had just finished *War and Peace* (in Russian!) and contended that it was the greatest book ever written.

"It says everything about everything," she gushed. "I only wish this war would end with a spirit of rejuvenation."

"I'm sure it will," I said, taking her hand. "We're not so old, you know."

"That's easy for you to say. A woman at forty, especially if she has grown children, can't expect much rejuvenation. She gets older, that's all."

I laughed heartily. "And a man in his midfifties? What about him?"

"Men are different," she replied.

"*Et vive la . . .*"

Her eyes twinkled. She was half teasing. "Have you read Darwin?"

"A little."

"Do you know he says that humans are the only species whose females live beyond the age of childbearing? Why do you suppose that is?"

"To keep old males happy." I patted her hand. "Come, dear, you're beautiful, and spring is a time for rejuvenation. Pass me another bit of chicken, will you?"

She was about to answer, when I saw a movement in the woods at the other side of the pond. "Shh," I whispered, "what's that?"

She turned to look. "*Merde.* People."

We'd almost finished eating, and Tania quickly gathered what food remained into the basket. She told me to grab the table and chairs and follow her a bit back into the woods.

"Come, come. *Vite! Vite! Vite!*"

She spread the cloth under a large oak tree. "I'm sorry, but I don't want to be bothered. Not today."

I didn't really mind, but I was curious about the other party. I sat with my back against the tree, positioned so that I could look across the pond to where the others were moving, still well back into the trees on their side. Tania opened me another beer and lay with her head in my lap.

"There," she sighed.

The others came down to a clearing on their side, and I

saw with some surprise that it was Lupa, Anna, and Watkins. Somehow I had never associated them with a picnic in the woods, but of course they were young and really much more likely than I to be enjoying a Sunday outdoors. They came into the clearing and set up chairs and a small table, and the two men sat down while Anna walked to the pond with a few bottles. She dropped them for chilling into the water.

"You know what I found interesting?"

I looked down at Tania. "What's that?"

"I found myself forgetting I was French. I despised the French, even though at the time I suppose I would have been as patriotic as I am now."

For some reason, this statement made absolutely no sense to me. Lupa and Watkins had set themselves up at their table—it looked as though they were about to play some board game—while Anna busied herself clearing a spot near the water. I took a sip of my beer and frowned.

"When?" I asked.

"The Napoleonic Wars. You couldn't help but want the Russians to win. It made me slightly uncomfortable while I was reading."

"Ah, *War and Peace*."

The two men across the pond were becoming engrossed in their game and rarely looked up, while Anna was busy making a small fire. Once Lupa called out to her loud enough so that we could hear his voice. At that, Anna got up and fetched the men some bottles from the pond, then went back to her work.

"I suppose we were wrong then."

"I don't believe we'd have thought so at the time," I said.

"But of course there are always reasons to start a war, just as there are more often than not no real reasons to end one. Everyone believes themselves right, which is probably understandable, but rather simple."

"You don't think we were right?"

"That depends. At that time I would have thought it, I'm sure. If your sons had been off fighting in Russia, you would never have given a thought to whether or not we were right. We would have *had* to have been right."

"Yes. I suppose so." She closed her eyes and breathed deeply. I thought she was going off to sleep. Anna had started to cook something over the fire, while the two men continued their game. The sun came down in patches there under the tree. It was beginning to get warm. Tania stirred and opened her eyes.

"But what about now?" she asked.

"What do you mean?"

"Are we right, now? Or will some German Tolstoy come along in fifty years and make us all appear to be beasts?"

"Whatever we may appear in fifty years," I said, "for the present time we're at least justified. France has to survive, and now it has to fight to survive." I leaned back and lit a cigarette. "Novelists make us think war is terrible because they tend to make a personal story out of it. Nationally, war is either desirable or necessary, never right or wrong. It's not a personal thing, any more than a storm is personal. If a bolt of lightning strikes down a man, no one says that there's any reason behind it. Some writers try to, saying it's an act of God or whatever, but that doesn't wash. It just happens, like war happens."

"But the people . . ."

"People don't matter in wars. Countries matter. Nations matter, issues matter. The last thing anyone should think about is people."

She closed her eyes again. "I think about my sons," she said, then added quietly, "all the time. And we both think of Marcel."

"But we don't know Marcel had anything to do with the war."

She looked up at me. "Don't we?"

I wondered how much she did know.

"And if he did have to do with the war, then he wouldn't matter, because people don't matter. Oh, Jules, you don't really believe that?"

I thought of the night before, and the reasons I had decided to stay on in Valence. I had let it become personal, which was absurd. France was what mattered. But finally I didn't believe that, and some sense of that realization had made me resign. I supposed I was, indeed, getting old. I touched Tania's face gently.

"No," I said, "I don't really believe that."

We were silent.

Across the pond nothing changed. I watched for several minutes, after which Watkins, evidently beaten in the game—I heard his "Damn!" clearly—abruptly stood up and stalked over to the fire.

"You know who that is over there?"

Tania sat up. "Who?"

"Your friend Lupa."

"*Your* friend Lupa," she said, frowning. "I'm surprised he had the energy to get all the way out here."

"It's not that he lacks energy—he just chooses a bit carefully how he wants to expend it."

"Well, let's not expend any of ours by calling him."

"I had no intention of doing that, my dear." I leaned over and kissed her.

She stood up. "Would you excuse me for a minute?" she asked.

She walked back a ways into the woods while I sat propped against the tree, watching the scene across the pond. Anna was removing something from the fire, while Lupa was putting up the game pieces and clearing the table. Anna went back to the pond for more bottles.

I took a drink of my beer, long and refreshing, closing my eyes and letting the cold liquid run down my throat. Suddenly there was a loud report. Opening my eyes, I saw Lupa and Watkins drop to the ground, while Anna screamed as she fell, rolling over and over. Behind me, I heard Tania call out my name, and I turned to see her running toward me. There were two more shots.

"You're all right?" I yelled, and she said she was. The shots I'd heard had been the loud ringing noises of a rifle rather than the soft pops of a pistol, so the range could have been great.

I took out my pistol. Tania came up to me. "You're not going—" she began.

I cut her off. "Go see to Anna. I think she's been hit."

"But Jules, you're not . . ."

I was already moving back toward the road, where the

shots had originated. Retired or not, I was a trained operative of the French government and knew how to act around
hostile elements. Perhaps I was curt to Tania, but such times
call for action, not sensitivity.

No more than a minute had passed since the third shot.
As I ran, I saw out of the corner of my eye another figure
moving through the woods to my left. It was Lupa, outpacing
me as we sprinted.

We broke from the woods at about the same time, all the
while moving rapidly toward the road, where we could see a
figure retreating into the trees on the other side toward my
house. Lupa fell momentarily from my vision, but, seconds
later, he appeared at my side astride one of the dray horses.

"Get up!"

His hand grabbed me like a vice as I bounded up behind
him. "Over there," I yelled, pointing to a break in the copse
just beyond the road. Lupa, holding the horse's mane, leaned
into the untrained beast and miraculously was obeyed.

I still held my pistol in my hand, dismally aware of its in-
adequacy. We were closing on the roadway and within another minute might expect to come upon our assailant, fleeing
on foot. It was not to be, however, as over the sound of the
horse's hooves we heard a motor turning over and saw, not
fifty meters away, an automobile kicking up dust as it spun
from its hiding place into the road.

I fired one ineffectual shot—from that range, the gesture
was about the equivalent of shouting "Stop!"—but Lupa
didn't hesitate. He spurred the horse back a bit to our right,
directly toward my house.

"Your car!" he yelled over his shoulder.

"*Tout droit!* Straight ahead." I pointed to the barn.

The car we'd seen had been covered, so we had no opportunity to see the driver or even whether there had been more than one occupant. Still, I would recognize the automobile itself—made of a corrugated iron just becoming popular here and painted a dull green.

We came to the barn and dismounted roughly. I stumbled and fell dismounting, but Lupa did not slow up at all. As I picked myself up, he was pulling back the building's door, grunting with the exertion. I ran past him and threw myself behind the wheel.

It pays to keep one's machinery in top condition, as I had done. Immediately, the motor caught, I slammed the gearshift into position and nearly ran over Lupa as the car lurched forward. He caught the windshield and leapt onto the running board, barely clearing the doorway.

I pressed the hand throttle to its limit, and before we had left my property, we were closing on fifty kilometers per hour. On the unpaved and pitted drive, the ride shook my very bones. I hoped the automobile would handle the shocks better.

"Anna?" I began.

"Not now!" Lupa bellowed.

As soon as we hit the road, however, it became smoother. The car skidded slightly as we turned left, and I nearly lost control of the wheel, but Lupa grabbed it and righted me as we continued our acceleration.

We hadn't gone a kilometer, though, when the ride very nearly ended. What I thought at first was a backfire, or perhaps a blowout, made me lean forward against the steering wheel. That move may have saved my life. Lupa, without the worry of watching the road, spun and evidently made out a glint of metal in another stand of trees by the road. It had been another shot.

"Keep driving," he yelled as I began to slow down. "Let Watkins get him."

"Are you sure?" I asked.

"Our man's in the car." he said. "Drive!"

Lupa pulled a weapon from under his coat. The pistol, an M-1911 Colt American military issue .45 automatic, boomed like a cannon as he fired off four rounds with what seemed to be impossible rapidity, the smoking brass jackets flying out the side of the weapon and onto the road. The fire was returned as we heard one more report from behind us.

"Damn!" Lupa spun around, grabbing his cheek. A sliver of red appeared and he wiped at it with his hand.

"You all right?"

"Scratched. Nothing more."

No more than three minutes had elapsed between the enemy's car breaking from the cover of the trees and our turning into the road in pursuit. With the speed of my Model T, if the chase lasted more than fifteen kilometers, I thought we had a chance of overtaking our prey. I kept the accelerator jammed to the floor while Lupa dabbed at the cut on his face with a handkerchief. Just as I turned to look his way and question him again about the initial shooting and how badly Anna had been hurt, we crested a small hill and I was forced to skid again, braking hard, as we came upon a horse-drawn produce cart from the other direction. We barely missed it as we screeched to a stop.

The driver had leapt off the cart to the roadside and lay sprawled in the shallow grass. "Has there been another car?" I asked.

Clearly furious, swearing violently, he seemed inclined to rush us. Lupa pointed his gun at the man's head and quieted him. "Has there been another car?"

"*Oui.*"

"How many passengers?"

The man shrugged. "I didn't notice," he said. "I was getting out of the way." In spite of Lupa's weapon, his anger spewed over again. "You bastards don't own the road, you know. I'm reporting this. I . . ."

We couldn't stay to discuss the niceties of *priorité à droit*, but pressed onward. If we were having trouble making headway, perhaps we were not alone.

The top was still off on the Model T, and the wind brought tears to my eyes, slightly impairing my vision. I didn't mind it, pushing the car to nearly 120 Ks. Very few other machines could match that speed. The road's surface, relatively smooth, nevertheless provided its share of bumps and necessitated my full attention.

Lupa stemmed the flow of his blood, then removed the clip from his weapon and refilled it. To my inquiring look, he answered, "We could have hurt him. The range is close to fifty meters."

"Who do you think it might have been?" I asked.

"I don't know." He dabbed again at his cheek reflectively. "I just don't know. Perhaps Watkins will come up with something."

I finally got the question out. "Anna was all right?"

He shook his head wonderingly. "Again, just a scratch. We've been uncommonly lucky."

I thought of Marcel. Our luck had its limits.

Within moments, we were on the outskirts of Valence. Cart traffic and a few military vehicles slowed our progress as we stopped and started, honking, through the narrow streets. The town was a maze of alleys, any one of which could hide the man we sought. But we had no choice other than to pursue his logical path—toward St. Etienne.

The frustrating ride through the city streets, where we were stopped time and again by carriages, children, geese, dogs, and pedestrians, continued and continued. Our only hope was that the car we followed was experiencing similar delays.

Finally, just as we broke from the confines of the cobbled streets and onto the smoother, wider thoroughfare that led to St. Etienne, Lupa grabbed my arm and cried out.

"There it is!"

I didn't know how he could be sure. The car was a mere speck on the roadway, and he'd only glimpsed it before it rounded a curve and disappeared again. Still, it was not a time to quibble, and I pushed the Ford to its limit.

We were gaining. As we took the same curve, we'd picked up perhaps fifty meters. Now, clearly, even to my blurred vision, it looked like the same car.

"Keep low," Lupa cautioned. "They might shoot."

I followed his instructions, and we closed rapidly. In another minute, we were within range of Lupa's weapon, but he held his fire. It would not be wise to shoot until we had seen the occupants.

By the time we reached the first aqueduct crossing the

Rhone, we had nearly come upon them, and it was becoming obvious to me that something had gone wrong. They were not pulling away, not shooting. In fact, they paid us no attention whatsoever.

As we pulled alongside, we glanced over at them—two elderly men in officer's uniforms. They looked back at us with mild curiosity, nothing more. At the first opportunity, I turned into a side road, drove on for several hundred meters, then pulled over.

"What now?" I asked.

The breeze blew over us gently. Overhead, a flock of birds chided us with their song.

· 11 ·

"We're fools," Lupa said.

"What else could we have done?"

"Yes. I'm trying to determine that now."

"There must be a dozen look-alike cars on the road."

"Jules," he explained, "I know the answers as well as you do. We must be asking the wrong questions."

We continued in frustrating and desultory conversation until, in the end, he asked if I would drop him off at La Couronne on my way back home.

"Aren't you curious about Anna?" I asked.

"I am many things in relation to her," he answered, "but almost never am I curious. No, I am sure she has gone back to be ministered to by Madame Chessal. She was fine, Jules, as fine as I am now. I did make sure before I joined with you."

The drive continued in silence. Occasionally I would

glance over at my companion. He sat, motionless, eyes closed, pursing his lips in and out. Finally, he spoke:

"Where was Madame Chessal when you heard the shots?"

"With me. Well, she'd gone off into the bushes for a moment."

"So she was not with you."

"Auguste, don't be absurd. She didn't even know we'd be here. She was nowhere near where the shots came from."

He looked at me in exasperation. "There is such a thing as a paid assassin. She wouldn't have to be where the shots came from."

I thought he was stretching the point beyond credibility and told him so.

"Jules," he said, "there are two kinds of women: simple women, accounting for ninety percent of the race, and dangerous women."

If he was brooding, I'd let him brood. I was convinced that his line of reasoning led nowhere, and nothing he said was going to shake that conviction. He seemed to come to the same conclusion, for suddenly he sat up straight in his seat.

"I apologize about the way I spoke of Madame Chessal. I still can't help but feel a great deal of mistrust, but with no evidence, I'm a fool to speak rashly. Forgive me." He sighed, back to business. "I've decided something rather crucial."

"What's that?"

"What did you see, exactly, when you heard the shots today?"

"Actually, I saw nothing. Just at the moment I heard the shots, I was tipping my head back to drink some beer. I saw nothing at all. Just before that, I saw Anna crossing back to the table and you and Watkins—no, just you—seated, presumably waiting for her."

"Correct. Does that lead you to note any similarity between this latest incident and the successful attempt on Routier?"

I couldn't see what he was getting at.

"Let me describe to you what happened today. Exactly. Anna had been at the fire getting our food and had turned back to the table. Watkins stood on the far side of the table, having just returned also from the fire. When the shot came, we were all precisely in a line from the direction of the report. Anna was grazed while leaning over to place the food on the table, and the same bullet passed through the bottom of Watkins's coat. I heard the whistle of the thing as it passed my ear. There! What does that tell you?"

"Nothing," I said truthfully. "Except perhaps that they're both very lucky."

"How about if they were both extremely unlucky? What if the bullet hadn't been meant for either of them?"

I smiled. "What if you are getting upset and nervous and losing your judgment?"

Ignoring that response, he continued. "The most salient point of these two attempts, last week's and today's, is that both attempts were on my own life. Of course, there is a possibility that this was not the case last Wednesday but only the barest possibility. You see—and I don't know whether you noticed this at the time—Routier, after the incident with Lavoie's bottle exploding, went back to the seat I'd been occupying and drank from my already poured glass. The poison had obviously been put there for me; only the chance realignment of our positions saved me and resulted in your friend's death.

"Again today," he went on, "today we were all in a line, and the shot chanced to miss me. You heard the other two? After the first we all dropped immediately to the ground. The second shot landed somewhere far off, but the last hit the ground not one meter from where I lay, which was far from the other two. No, whoever the killer may be, the intended victim is beyond dispute. It is myself. And whatever else the killer may be, we may be certain that he's getting desperate."

"All right," I said, after a moment, "it might be true. And if it is, what are you going to do?" I negotiated back onto the cobblestones. In contrast to our earlier passage *en ville*, no one seemed to be about.

"I'd like you to go and find out where Pulis was today. Then go to the police station, find where Lavoie is supposed to be, and wire him. As I said, it's possible that there's a hired assassin involved, even though further reflection renders that rather dubious. A hired assassin wouldn't have missed me, and if our man was so concerned about covering up, he certainly wouldn't have done anything at your house the other night. No, I believe he's acting alone on this. I believe he's scared, and a scared man makes mistakes."

"What about Paul?"

"Anser? You're going to see him tomorrow, are you not?"

"Yes."

"Well . . . question him. Find out what you can. Watkins, remember, will be working in St. Etienne."

"All right, but you?"

"I'm going back to La Couronne. I don't intend to leave my rooms until this is cleared up. A scared man, as I said, makes mistakes. I can't be wondering about my own safety if I'm to be effective. My cooking, too, is suffering. As you see, I should be there now. Charles is no chef, but he's taking over when he can. I try to show him a style, but how do you teach a flair, eh? Monsieur Vernet, La Couronne's owner, is very patient. We are, in fact, distantly related. He is a good man, but he is also a businessman, a restaurateur. He needs a quality chef to survive. Much as I need a quality operative." He glanced sideways at me. "Would you object to filling that role?"

I could not. It was flattering—but more, necessary. If Lupa was right, then he, not I, was in danger.

"Jules, stop the car!" he said suddenly.

We were passing the fountain in the center of town, from which side streets spread like spokes from a wheel. I pulled over to the curbside and brought the car to a halt.

"What is it?"

"Come with me."

Lupa was already out of the car, his hand inside his coat near his pistol. He disappeared down one of the alleys. Moving as quickly as I could, I followed. The run through the woods, the horse ride, my stumbling, the excitement of the chase—all of that was catching up with me. In the leisurely pace of the drive back to Valence, I had stiffened up considerably. But I was not about to let myself forget that I'd kept up with a man not yet half my age. I thought confidently that Lupa could pick a worse operative than myself.

Rounding the corner, I saw what had drawn Lupa's attention. A green automobile of corrugated iron was pulled up under an overhanging gutter. The driver's window was open, and Lupa had already entered the car by the time I arrived.

"Anything?"

He straightened up in the seat, smiling crookedly. Opening his hand, he displayed one spent rifle shell. "Nothing important," he said. "Perhaps you ought to file a report on a stolen car. I'm sure the owner of this machine is wondering where it might be."

He got out of the car. "I might as well walk from here, Jules. Thank you for your help." He nodded and began down the alley. Then he stopped, turning. "I suppose for form's sake I should ask Watkins to question the residents of this block. They may have seen . . ."

Then, abruptly, his shoulders slumped. "This is terrible. My mind isn't functioning. The police will not be able to discover who stole this car. No one will have seen it arrive here. . . . Our function is not pedestrian police work. We cannot depend on that, for if we do we shall fail. Mark my words, we shall fail!"

I tried to calm him, to restore some of his lost self-esteem. It did little good. Finally, I assured him that I would check in on Anna, though he didn't even seem to think that would be necessary. He said I could do as I wished.

As I trudged back to my car, I wondered if even now our assailant was watching me from one of the narrow windows, gloating over his escape. Whoever he was, it was likely that he knew me well and thought me a bumbling adversary, a foolish dilettante, an aging clown.

· 12 ·

All the shops had been closed on Sunday, and Henri had bickered with his wife and gone fishing alone. No one had seen him. He'd caught no fish, though when he returned, his boots had been wet. Tuesday, tomorrow, he would be making a delivery of condiments to St. Etienne. When I saw him Monday morning, I learned all this. He was nervous as usual, but sober, and I only stayed a moment on the pretext of having forgotten something.

I then sent a telegram to Avignon, where, according to the list he'd left with the police, Georges should have been staying. I expected no reply until evening at the earliest.

It was a cool and overcast day. The changes in weather had been abrupt, but one expected that in the spring. Perhaps the clouds would burn off by the afternoon.

I walked from the telegraph office to Lupa's with my hands thrust deep into the pockets of my overcoat, seeing no one on my way.

He sat enthroned in his office. That's the only way to describe him. So he had abandoned his schedule. It was after ten o'clock, and by all rights, he should have been up on the street with beer and newspaper. As it was, he sat behind his huge desk with the paper open before him and a glass by his left hand.

"Hello," I said, sitting down. I'd asked Charles for coffee on the way through the kitchen and awaited him. "So you've given up working altogether."

"I beg your pardon." He looked up.

"You look so settled there, it's hard to imagine that you'll ever move back to the world of labor."

"Cooking is not a labor but a love. I intend to continue with my duties here." He put the paper aside. "You've read that Italy has joined us? That, at least, is good news. How are you today?"

I told him about Pulis and the telegram while Charles was pouring my coffee. He listened with his eyes closed, leaning back far in his chair. When I had finished, he frowned.

"It would make things much easier if we could ever eliminate someone completely. You say he's going to St. Etienne tomorrow?"

As I nodded, there was a loud, ringing alarm. Lupa reached to a button on his desk and pressed it, shutting off the noise. He calmly opened his desk and took out his pistol, checking to see that it was loaded. "Stay here," he said to me and disappeared into the tunnel. I sat uncomfortably for several minutes before I heard returning footsteps and voices. The curtain came aside and Lupa reentered with Watkins.

". . . So it seems possible, though rather a long shot," said the Englishman as he came into the room. "Ah, hello. I didn't realize you were here."

"He's only just arrived," said Lupa. "Would you have some coffee? Tea?"

"Tea, please."

"Fine." He ordered it, and we waited.

"Excuse me," I said, "but what seems possible?"

Lupa closed his paper. "Joseph here has just returned from St. Etienne, where he's been trying to find some information we can use. He's not working at all on the murders, as you are, but only on the arsenal. After the attempt yesterday, I thought things would start to move quickly, but I was wrong. Nothing happened, at least that we know of, at St. Etienne. Joseph believes, however, that he was followed for quite some time, even back here to Valence, possibly by the man who shot at us. He was about to describe him."

Watkins slouched in his chair, looking rather ragged, as though he hadn't slept. The tea arrived, and he sipped at it. Suddenly, when he was about to speak, his eyes became illuminated, and he lost his vacant look. It was amazing, almost as though he were two different people.

"Actually, I never did get a good look at his face. He had brownish hair, I think, dressed plainly, about six foot." He smiled. "Brilliant description, what? Could as well be me I'm talking about." Then he shifted back into himself and sat as though he'd been deflated, sipping at his tea. "God, I'm tired."

"Why don't you get yourself some sleep? Are you going back to St. Etienne right away?"

"I thought I'd go down a bit later, say after dark."

Lupa nodded. "Satisfactory. I'm getting ready to move, to

create something if necessary. I've got a good guess who we want. By the way, Pulis is coming down tomorrow morning to deliver. Watch him." He turned to me. "How does he go down?"

"Produce cart, I imagine."

"Good, then he'll be easy to pick up. Catch him outside of town and follow him everywhere. If he meets anyone . . . well, do what you can. It would be nice if we could use the police."

Watkins stood and moved to the door. "Got it."

"This trip back and forth must get tedious. When you go down, stay until you have something. I have a feeling things are coming to a head."

"Yes, sir," he said and started out.

"Oh, Watkins!"

He stopped and looked back in.

"Don't you think it might be better if you exited the same way you entered? It's just possible that someone might notice you coming out of a building you'd never entered. Also, in the future, why not try coming in by way of the restaurant."

"Right, right, right . . ." he muttered, crossing the room again. "The plants need watering. I've turned on the lights." He left.

"No olives?" I asked.

"Certainly an oversight. Is there anything else?"

"I was wondering where Anna fits in. In fact, I've wondered about where all of us fit in. I get the distinct impression that there are things you'd rather I knew nothing about, and I'd like to know why."

He sighed. "You're right. There is much you don't need to know. Ideally, you wouldn't know Watkins, but there's no harm in that. For the other things, wait a few more days. You might treat people differently if you knew their alignment with us. For now, you know enough to do your job."

"Well, then, Anna at least . . ."

"Yes?"

"I'd like to know if Tania's in danger with her being there, or if that was arranged by you."

"Oh, no. Certainly not. I'm concerned, in fact, about any danger Anna may be in."

"Not that again."

"No," he said. "No, not that again. We are simply in different camps on that question, and I'm afraid it won't be resolved until I've seen Madame Chessal's family, perhaps until the whole matter is closed. But Anna . . . I don't know what to do about her."

"Is she with us?"

"Not in the sense you mean. I've gotten myself entangled with her. She knows generally what my functions are, and sometimes she's a great help, but she works for no government. I think when she leaves Madame Chessal's care, I'm going to send her away. We've talked of marriage."

"Congratulations."

"Posh! A man shouldn't be congratulated when he finds himself trapped. I feel I owe it to her, in a way. She's done a lot for me."

"But that's terrible!" I said. "Don't you love her at all?"

"Oh, love. Come, Jules, let's not be sentimental. Surely, I care for her, but I realize that these things pass. I'm too much my own man to tolerate a woman around for very long. Still"—he sighed—"she is a good woman. I suppose there's no help for it. I will send her away for a while." He sat back and closed his eyes. The alarm once more sounded.

"That would be Watkins again. I should show him the switch. Well?" he said after a pause. "Anything else?"

"Yes, there is. Talking of Anna just reminded me. I'm not working with the government.anymore. I've resigned."

He opened his eyes a fraction. "Hmmm . . ."

"I expect there'll be some trouble."

"Undoubtedly. Why?"

"Transfer."

"The fools! Don't they believe there's trouble here? Their own agents are dying consistently. So you've quit. Well, good. I'll see if I'll be able to assuage some of their more re- taliatory instincts. Don't worry."

"I wasn't," I said, getting up.

"Fine. Wednesday night?"

"Oh, yes, all set with Henri and Tania. Georges said any- where would be all right with him, and I'm going to see Paul now, so I'll let you know. Oh, one more thing: the po- lice want to see me. They've possibly seen me come here. How well do I know you?"

"Slightly."

"Good, that'll be easy, then. I'll see them this afternoon after I get back." So saying, I turned and left, hearing him calling for Charles to bring more beer.

I'd left the car parked at the telegraph office, so I walked back to it in the still brisk morning, trying again to piece together all I'd seen and heard, and once again coming up with a blank.

Since I'd never been to Paul's house, I had a little trouble getting to it and was totally unprepared for what greeted me. It was set back on a small trail, nearly a kilometer from any real road, and looked like something from a fairy tale. It was tiny and seemed to be perfectly square, no more than ten meters on a side, though it did have two stories. I'd needed to ask directions before I arrived from some children who were playing nearby. All of them knew the place and seemed surprised that I didn't. The roof was sharp-sloping, of the kind you see more often in Switzerland, though it was shingled with the familiar red tile. The house itself was white.

I parked to one side of the trail, walked to the small door, and knocked.

"*Entrez! Un moment.*" Paul's voice came from upstairs. "*Qui est la?*"

"It's Jules," I answered, sitting down. "No hurry."

The first thing I noticed about the inside was the cats. There were seven different kinds of felines lounging over the sparse furniture. I'd never supposed that Paul was so fond of cats; he'd never mentioned them, as cat lovers are generally wont to do. I, personally, did not particularly like them. The other outstanding feature of the room was the plants. There were potted plants in every window and suspended from the ceiling. "Well," I said to myself, "after all, he is a poet."

As though on cue, Paul came down the stairs.

"Jules, good to see you. What brings you around?" We shook hands. His was rather clammy. He was wearing American blue denims and a shirt he called his *chemise de l'Ouest*, a white affair with sloping pockets and mother-of-pearl buttons. "I'm just making some lunch. Will you have some?"

"Just coffee would be fine, thanks."

He walked back to another room, which appeared to be no bigger than a closet. He called me in.

"You've never been here before, right? Right. Well, it surely won't do to have you leave without the grand tour. This room here's the kitchen."

Compared to my own kitchen, it didn't seem even minimally adequate for cooking. There were a pair of burners set on a drain and two or three shelves with a very few condiments lying in disarray upon them. The coffeepot was black with carbon, and looked as though it hadn't been cleaned, ever. There was no sink. He went outdoors to a pump for the water. On the walls were faded posters of Buffalo Bill Cody's Wild West Show and one of Ringling Bros. Barnum & Bailey Circus (The Greatest Show on Earth). He dumped several measures of coffee into the water and set the whole thing on a burner to boil. I wondered what Lupa would have had to say about the operation.

"Don't worry about the grounds, Jules. There's a filter inside the spout."

Not clearly reassured, I waited, making small talk until the water was boiling. He poured us two cups, took himself a bit of cheese, and we went back into the sitting room. As soon as he was settled, two cats came and sat on his lap, and as we talked, he broke off bits of the cheese and fed them.

"Now," he said again, "what brings you round here?"

"I said I'd get back to you about Wednesday night. You think you'll be able to make it? We'd like to have it at La Couronne, since everyone feels the way you do about my place. What do you say?"

"Why'd you pick that place?"

"Monsieur Lupa offered it." I shrugged.

"He's coming again, is he?"

"Yes. He said we could use his kitchen, which is large and private. I've already sent over lots of beer. He seems anxious to meet us all under better conditions, and I've talked to him once or twice since . . . since Wednesday."

"Why's he so anxious to get together with us again?"

"I don't know. He didn't really say that. I just got the impression."

"Hmm . . ." He drank the coffee, which wasn't, finally, as bitter as I'd expected. "Seems a mite strange. But then . . ."

"*He* is, as you say, a mite strange. But then, I've never been here before, and I find it quite, er, unorthodox. I've never really trusted men who liked cats, if you'll pardon me for saying so. And I find it funny that I've known you all this while, and never would have suspected that of you."

He smiled. "Well, do you trust me less now?"

"It's really not a question of trust or mistrust. I simply find it odd that your fondness for cats doesn't somehow show. Cats seem more of a woman's pet, and you're certainly not what I'd call effeminate."

"Shucks, no." He laughed out loud now, nudging the cats playfully behind their heads. "Well, now you know I like cats, but that doesn't show any more than if I smoked hashish or wore buffalo skin underwear, which, by the way, I don't."

I sipped at my coffee. "Well, yes, but . . ."

"No. You just can't tell. Take all this stuff about Marcel.

Now, I'm sorry and all to see him dead, and I'm sorry for you because you were his friend, but how much did we know about him? Hell, I didn't even know where he lived. What if, for example—and don't get mad—he was having an affair with Tania, and you found out and killed him. Or if he had recently gambled everything on some adventure, and lost, and for that reason killed himself. No way to know. Or if he was a spy of some kind, like some of the others said, and the whole thing had nothing at all to do with him personally, though I myself don't credit that one much. He just didn't seem the cloak-and-dagger type. 'Course, there I go again doing what I'm yappin' at you about. He didn't seem the cloak-and-dagger type, and I don't seem the cat-lover type, though I am, isn't that right, Esau?" This last was addressed to the large black tom seated sedately on his lap. "When you come down to it, and be honest, would I strike you as a poet?"

"I must admit . . . no. Though more so here in your house than elsewhere."

"Because here I'm more eccentric?"

"I suppose, yes."

"But that's just another cliché, you see. The eccentric, sensitive poet. I lived just this way for years before I wrote my first poem. Cats, plants, and all. You want some more coffee?" I shook my head no, but he got up and walked to the kitchen for some of his own. He yelled from there. "Gotta brew up some more. It'll be a minute."

I saw Paul walking outside toward the pump. At the same time, one of the small kittens jumped from a chair and scampered to the foot of the narrow staircase. When I moved to see it more clearly, it bolted up the stairs, then turned to look back at me. Alarmed at the height it had attained, it began whining piteously, and I got up intending to hold it until Paul's return.

But I must have spooked it again, because it turned and disappeared up into a room at the top of the stairs. In all innocence, I followed it into Paul's bedroom-cum-workspace, with a cluttered desk and an unmade bed. Over the bed were more dusty prints of American shows, and the wall over the desk was covered with books along its entire length and breadth. There were two large windows, one just to each side of the bed, and in the corner a stepladder leading to a square hole in the ceiling.

Forgetting the cat and feeling guilty, I nevertheless crossed to the desk and silently opened the top center drawer. It was filled with well-nibbled pencils, yellowing bits of paper with fading snatches of writing barely visible—in short, exactly what should have been there. Glancing at the books in front of me, I found the titles entirely commensurate with my expectations. Possibly he had a hollow book up there, but suddenly that struck me as highly unlikely. The room just didn't *feel* like a hiding place, and I was beginning to feel foolish and slightly embarrassed for having invaded Paul's privacy.

He would be returning shortly with his coffee, and I resolved to get back downstairs as quickly as I could, when the kitten whined again, this time from the hole in the ceiling. Somehow it had made it up the stepladder and now was truly frightened. I moved over and looked up while the crying continued.

"Come here, kitty," I said, my foot poised on the bottom

rung. As I've mentioned, I'm not much of a cat person, and my technique in calling was not effective. In fact, the animal disappeared back into the opening. "Come on," I repeated. "Good kitty, come here." I climbed the few steps and looked around.

As my eyes became adjusted to the darkness, I was dumbfounded by what I saw. The attic looked like an arsenal. The walls on both sides under the pitched eaves were covered with rifles and pistols of every size and description. The cat forgotten, I crawled up into the small space and stared. Boxes of ammunition for the various guns sat open on the floor. I noticed a few bullet molds near a low table, what appeared to be a lead smelter, cleaning rags, the usual paraphernalia.

In my shock, I must have lost track of the time. Paul's voice echoed faintly from below, and then almost immediately I heard his bounding footsteps on the stairs. I had no time to cover my indiscretion.

"I'm up here, Paul," I said feebly, "in the attic."

"What the hell . . . ?" he began.

I looked down at him. "I was trying to rescue a cat."

As though on cue, the kitten crawled to the opening and looked over, meowing at the sight of its owner.

Paul stood on the balls of his feet as though poised for action, the coffee steaming in his right hand. I watched his face carefully and even went so far as to make sure my own pistol was within easy reach. But after a moment of consternation, he seemed to reach some decision and smiled at me, his insouciant air returning.

"Well," he said, "I guess you've found me out."

"I had no idea you had such an interest in guns."

He grinned. "Another surprise. First cats, then plants, now guns."

"But so many?"

He shrugged. "It's a hobby."

"You'll pardon me if I say it's a strange hobby, especially at this time. Do the police know about it?"

"I doubt it," he said, "or they'd have probably arrested me in spite of the fact that Marcel was poisoned."

"But what do you do with them?"

"I save them, shoot them, clean them, make ammo. It relaxes me. Takes my mind off the jungle of literary life. Besides, guns fascinate me, always have."

"Aren't you worried about being discovered?"

"God! You talk as though I'd done something. No, not at all. I never let the kids up here, of course, and the few friends to whom I've shown the place can be trusted. I figure if you can trust me with your beer, the least I can do is reciprocate. No, I'm not worried."

"Do you shoot them often?"

"Sure. In fact, yesterday I packed a few of 'em away and went off shooting. Got a couple of rabbits, though I got the first one with a buffalo gun. If there weren't so many of the damn pests, I suppose I'd feel unsportsmanlike, but it's good practice."

"Are you a good shot?"

"In all modesty, Jules, I am a crack shot."

"Yet another thing I'd never have guessed."

"Amazing, isn't it? And there's probably a lot more. I've got quite a few tricks up my sleeve. You know, I was in Alaska when I was a boy, looking to get rich on gold. Picked

up a lot of useful knowledge there, not to mention most of
my adult interests. Probably that's why I like the kids here so
much and take the time for them. Lots of old men helped
me out up there, and it wasn't so easy to get by." He stopped
abruptly, remembering, drinking his coffee reflectively, his eyes
far away. "But come, Jules, take a look at what I really do."

I had to turn my back to him to come down the ladder
and I felt a surge of trepidation as I began, but it was quickly
over. He led me to the desk and picked up one of the stacks
of paper, covered with what was, to me, an illegible scrawl.
Americans write in a strange hand.

"My first retrospective," he said proudly. "Collected best
poems from my other books. They're even allowing me to
pick the material. I'm a little nervous because I've decided to
include twenty-three new poems. They asked for a collection of published stuff."

I picked up the bundle. "Looks like a lot of work, but it's
impressive, Paul. I'm sure they won't mind the new work."

"I don't really see why they would, but you never know."

"You know," I said, "I'd like to read your work correctly
translated someday. I always enjoy it but I'm afraid I miss nu-
ances in English. And the poetry must be very good if they
want a collection."

He shrugged. "It's a living. Beats looking for gold." He sat
in the chair behind the desk and stared out the window. "I
understand, though, that this will be translated into French,
so you may get your chance. I'll autograph a copy for you."

I thanked him and saw an opening for more questioning.
"Where do you get your ideas, Paul? What does a poet do
on an average day?"

The subject seemed to interest him. "Yesterday wasn't my average day, what with the shooting and all, and neither is today, since you've come. But generally I get up around dawn and drink coffee, write for two hours, and go after food. When I get back I have lunch, then go up to the studio and work on my hobbies. Usually, the kids come by. I'm kind of the neighborhood character. They all love coming over here, and we go out and fool around, exploring or whatever. One of the boys got a motorcycle not so long ago, and we've been doing a lot of fooling with that. Lots of fun. You ever ride one? No? Well, you wouldn't believe the speed. Then I generally go to town and have dinner with one of my friends, then home, a little more writing, and bed. Doesn't sound eccentric, does it?"

"Not to me," I admitted. I stood up and walked over to the plants. "You know one of Lupa's fetishes is plants, too?"

"See?" He came over to where I stood and began plucking dead leaves from some stems. "I never would have figured that."

"*Mais c'est vrai,*" I said. "Have you heard anything new about Marcel's death?"

"Have they arrested someone? I'd be happy to see that. It's a real pain reporting every day to the *flics.*"

"No. One of the investigators has been found dead."

He went to a chair and sat down.

"Well, I'm damned! Looks like a bad business."

"Very," I agreed. "He'd just been to see Henri."

"The poor bastard! You think he did it?"

"I've no idea. I'm trying to keep out of it as much as I can. Haven't seen the police yet."

"Probably a good idea. In fact, thinking about it, I'm not sure if it's such a good idea meeting with everyone on Wednesday. Why not put it off a week?"

"I should give you a reason, but it's really more of a personal thing with me. We've, most of us, been friends for so long that I thought it would be good to get back together, lay any suspicion to rest."

"You're right, I suppose. It *would* be good to see everyone back to normal." He stood again with his coffee cup in his hand and clapped me heartily on the back. "Well, Jules, rest assured. I don't suspect you of anything, except that I instinctively mistrust cat haters." He laughed.

"Then can I expect you on Wednesday?"

"Sure as shootin'."

"Comment?"

"That means, yes, count on it."

"Ah." I nodded. "Have a good day. *Ciao.*"

Paul showed me out, and I walked back to the car. He had raised many more questions for me than he'd answered. He'd been out yesterday with a rifle. But of course, if he were a crack shot, he wouldn't have missed. Then again, possibly . . .

Hell, I thought, possibly anything.

I got in the car and started off toward the road. I rounded a turn and came upon a group of youths running alongside a boy on a motorbike, heading back toward Paul's house. It was still a bit chilly, and I'd left my windows up, so that as I passed the boys their voices were muffled and indistinct, though shrill, and blended with the noise of the motor. I had the uneasy feeling that I'd heard those same voices before.

· 13 ·

Jacques Magiot and I had been acquaintances for over forty years, and a mutual antipathy had developed between us over the course of time. When he was beginning his career with the police, I was a gadabout. He was a few years older than I, and before we'd finished *secondaire*, we'd had many of the same friends. Our fathers, as a matter of fact, had been quite close. After they had retired, they spent most of their afternoons together playing *boules*. So it was more or less assumed that we would become friends. It never happened. Once he tried to recruit me to the force, and I'd laughed at the notion. From that time, the condescension with which he'd always treated me—friendly condescension, to be sure—turned to subtle derision. I think he always considered me a do-nothing, and it no doubt angered him when I began to increase my father's already substantial fortune through my own resources. Still, we would meet at parties occasionally and exchange pleasantries. As a policeman, he was competent for routine problems, entirely without imagination, and through some admixture of luck and obstinancy had arrived at the position of police chief of Valence.

The police headquarters building was a large neoclassic monstrosity in the center of town. Arched and pillared, it might have been made by a blind, one-armed Roman. It was the largest building in town, built *sans doute* on the theory that if might makes right, big makes beautiful. *Tant pis.*

I was ushered down the hall from the front desk to the room of one of the subordinates, a Monsieur Procunier. He was a short, heavy bald man with a large nose and a florid complexion. He sat behind his desk and bade me sit facing him.

"Nice of you to come," he began sarcastically. "We've been by your house several times. Have you received that message? There have been some murders lately, you realize."

I nodded. "My good man, Monsieur Magiot knows where he can find me, and no one said there was any urgency. Indeed, there couldn't have been, or you'd have stationed someone at the house and brought me here as soon as I appeared. Now I'm here, voluntarily, to answer questions, I presume, and I have little use for sarcasm. Let's get on with it." I smiled. "By the way, will Monsieur Magiot be in?"

"He's in now. He's to see you when I'm through taking your report."

"Fine. I'm at your disposal."

He asked me the same questions they'd asked the previous Wednesday, adding only a reference or two to Chatelet's death. Did I have any suspicions? Had anything out of the ordinary happened to me since Wednesday? I didn't know what Fritz might have told them, so I mentioned the episode with the rock and left out yesterday's shooting incident.

"You think it was a prank?" he asked.

"Without any doubt. I heard children's voices."

"Would you like a police escort?"

"Good God, no! Whatever for?"

"Protection."

So it went. How well did I know the people at the gathering? What was the purpose of the meeting? Did I know that if more than three people met at any time, it could be construed as a subversive gathering and was forbidden?

"Thank you," I said. "Is that all?"

He directed me to Magiot. Jacques was dealing with some of his men when I entered, and I stood quietly by the door while he finished talking with them. After they'd filed out, he reached out his hand.

"Jules," he said. "Good to see you. It's been quite a while. Nasty business, this, eh? I'm awfully sorry about Routier. He was a good friend of yours, I understand. Do sit down. Cigarette?"

He carried his age very well. Though he was not compelled to by regulations, he preferred to wear his uniform while on duty, and it was well tailored. His dark hair was in a military cut over a disciplined and impassive face. He sat gripping his pipe lightly with both hands over the bowl, his elbows resting on the desk.

I took the cigarette, and sat. "How are you, Jacques? Your man Procunier is quite a personality."

He waved it off. "Oh, sorry about that. I've just been so

busy lately I'd rather have him take the routine things. You made a statement?"

"*Oui.*"

"Good. To tell the truth, I was a little concerned about the circumstances of the death at your place. Several foreigners, that sort of thing. You know gatherings of that size are forbidden."

"To drink beer?"

"I know, I know. In your case, it's rather silly. But there are reasons, as I'm sure you'll understand. There have been rumors that Routier was mixed up in some international matters. Would you know anything about that?"

"Nothing whatever. We'd been friends for a long time, and he never mentioned anything to me. Also, Jacques, between us, he didn't really seem the type, did he?"

He smiled condescendingly. "Yes. Well, I thought I'd ask." He shifted in his chair and, looking down into the bowl of his pipe, said rather softly, "We think we know who did it."

"Really," I said. "Who?"

"How well do you know this Auguste Lupa? That was the first time he'd been to your house, wasn't it?"

"Not exactly. He'd been there that morning. As to how well I know him—hardly at all. I only met him last Tuesday, and he seemed a nice enough chap. He's really an excellent chef, you know."

"So I've heard. That's one of the reasons we find it strange he was there. He should be working at night. We've gone by La Couronne several times and have failed to find him. Why wouldn't he be there during working hours?"

"I don't know," I replied. "It does seem suspicious."

"Suspicious, ha! Damned suspicious, I'd say."

"But, Jacques, you haven't been able to get in touch with me either in all that time, and there's nothing suspicious about me, is there?"

"I hate to bring it up, Jules, but you don't work like your common man. Your hours are your own to order."

I smiled to myself. Probably my wealth would gall him forever. "So you suspect Lupa?"

"Look at the facts," he said. "Lupa's the only new man at the party. He's a foreigner, from Belgrade or somewhere—"

"He's an American citizen," I interrupted.

"All right, America. Doesn't change the fact. Then, Routier's sitting in Lupa's seat and even drinking from his glass when he keels over. Lupa hadn't even taken a sip from that glass. In the confusion of Lavoie's glass breaking, Lupa dumps cyanide into the glass and arranges it so that Routier goes back to his seat. We don't know exactly how he did that, but it seems reasonable. We've also got some problems with motive, though this international angle might come into play there. Then Lupa can't be found when we want him, he refuses to cooperate at all, and"—here he paused for effect—"we went to see Vernet, the owner of La Couronne, and got Lupa's papers, and they're forged. Cleverly, but definitely. We're going to pick him up tonight."

I sighed. "Well, that's certainly a relief, Jacques. I'm glad you've found him. It does look rather bad for him. Forged, you say?"

"Without doubt."

"What about your inspector? Him, too?"

"We think so. He's got no alibi. We figure Chatelet—that was his name—was on to something. He questioned Lupa, and Lupa panicked. With his size, he could have strangled him easily, and probably did. He hadn't reported back to us yet, but his itinerary that morning had him seeing Lupa after the funeral, then the others, and none of the others saw him. He must have seen Lupa first, and been killed before he could see anyone else."

"But couldn't it have happened that when Chatelet saw that Lupa'd missed the funeral, he changed his plans and took off on a new tack? In that case he might have run into someone else altogether."

"Yes, that's true. But why would he change his plans? Did anything strange happen at the funeral? Anything to make you suspicious?"

"No," I said truthfully.

"Well, then."

"Just a thought," I muttered.

"You just let us handle this, Jules. It's what we do best."

I got up to go. "Well, good luck, Jacques. I hope you get him. And thank you."

He shook my hand warmly. "It's a pleasure to set the mind of an old friend at ease. Don't worry about a thing. We'll have everything straightened out and back to normal in no time."

I walked out into the cool evening. If that was what they did best . . . I smiled grimly to myself. So no one else had seen Chatelet, which of course meant that Henri had lied to the police. Understandable, but certainly neither wise nor wily. I decided to go to Lupa's, to warn him. He wouldn't be any good at all from inside a jail trying to convince a man like Magiot of his innocence. Magiot thought I was supercilious. I shuddered to imagine what he'd think of Lupa.

It wouldn't do to go directly to La Couronne from the police station, so I walked to my car and drove several blocks back toward my house, checking to see that I wasn't being tailed, I wasn't. I parked and began walking, then, back in the direction of Anna's shop. I knew it was a bit risky entering that way, but it would be better than just dropping in, especially if the police had already arrived.

The walk took me nearly a quarter of an hour, and it was completely dark when I arrived. The door was locked, as I might have expected if I'd been thinking of details, such as Anna lying wounded at Tania's house, but it presented no problem. Once inside, I crossed to the back door, behind the screen, and opened it. The smell of the flowers rising to meet me was once again overpowering but pleasant as I picked my way back to the tunnel entrance. I remembered roughly where Lupa had reached to turn off the alarm and, after fumbling along the darkened wall for a short while, got it and clicked it to what I hoped was off. The walk was becoming nearly familiar, and I covered the distance to Lupa's room in less than five minutes. Magiot had said that they were picking up Lupa tonight, and it was now night. There wasn't much time to waste.

I stood at the curtains and listened to see if Lupa had guests. There was a faint glow around one edge of the curtain, so at least one of the room's lights was on. I heard no sound, so I quietly pulled the curtain open and stepped in. My training had not entirely deserted me, and I could still move quietly and effectively if I had to. Lupa sat at his desk, absorbed in some reading. He turned a page, and I cleared my throat.

Normally, a man surprised in that manner will start. Lupa didn't move a muscle. Without the merest glance at me, he closed the book and stared ahead of him. Finally, he turned his head to see me.

"How did you get in here?" he snapped.

"Spontaneous generation."

"How long have you been here?"

"Under a minute. Now relax. It was necessary. You're in a lot of trouble, and we've got to move right away."

"So the tunnel's been unguarded for ten minutes . . . *pfui*." He reached for the button on his desk and activated the alarm again.

"You can check all that later," I said. "Get Charles in here, and Vernet as soon as he can be reached. I've just come from the police, and you're to be arrested tonight for Marcel's murder."

He glared at me. "The fools!"

"I couldn't agree more, but that doesn't matter much at this point. We've got to get you out of here and covered before the police arrive."

"The fools!" he repeated.

"Yes," I said. "It seems that they've checked your papers and discovered the forgeries, and that Henri has denied seeing Chatelet, and naturally they assume, then, that you killed him before he could have seen anyone else. Now, does Charles know about the tunnel?"

"Yes. So does Vernet."

"Anyone else?"

"Besides you, Anna, Watkins, and myself? No. Not that I know of."

"All right. Let's get you out that way then. Call in your men."

"No," he said. "No, I'm not leaving here. Simply impossible. I'm a marked man, and I've decided to stick it out here, and I will do so. I'll call the others."

"But how—"

He cut me off by ignoring me and calling out into the kitchen. Charles appeared shortly, clad in an apron and chef's cap, smiling. He was surprised to see me, but nodded courteously.

Lupa began talking. "Close the front door immediately and go fetch Monsieur Vernet. We are closed for business tonight due to the loss of our chef. I beg your pardon, Charles, but it does have nothing to do with you. After you've gotten Vernet here, continue on out to Monsieur Giraud's house—you remember where it is? Good. Talk to his chef, a Fritz Benet, and tell him to stop whatever he is doing and come along here as quickly as possible. Tell him Monsieur Giraud is in trouble, and we need him. Bring him through the back way. Try to do all this in under an hour, and start now." Charles already had stripped himself of accoutrements and stood ready to go. Lupa turned to me. "You have a car, n'est-ce pas? Bien. Give the keys to Charles. You can drive, can't you? Use the car. Speed is everything. Va-t-en! Go!"

When he'd left, Lupa excused himself and left me sitting

wondering what he planned to do. I heard him moving about in the adjoining room, evidently rearranging things in some way. In a short while he reappeared, carrying two beers in each hand. He set them on his desk and opened two, offering one to me without a word. Then he sat with his eyes closed and breathed deeply for what seemed an hour but was actually probably less than a minute. Finally he sat up, opened his eyes, and glanced at the beer glass, presumably to see that the foam had settled adequately, and drank. When he put the glass down, it was empty, and he immediately reached for another beer. He looked at me after pouring.

"So."

"If you don't mind my asking, what are you planning to do? You can't stay here, and every minute we sit here threatens you more. Why don't we just go over to my place, or at least through the tunnel? Here you are too vulnerable."

"Nonsense. What I did in the outer room just then will prevent any interference from the police. The huge tapestries covering the other walls? Well, for such an eventuality as this, I've another on hand. I've simply covered the door to the office and the wall surrounding it. No one will suspect there is a room there."

"But if they search, it's transparent."

"Why would they search? If they're capable of thinking me guilty of Marcel's death, they are no danger to me. They will look in the rooms that remain, which are certainly ample for one man living alone. They won't suspect a hidden room. Why should there be one? Monsieur Vernet will tell them he fired me because of my papers, and Charles will corroborate. Then, of course, there will be a new chef, newly hired, and living in these quarters."

"I suppose that would be . . ."

"Exactly. Fritz." He drank more beer, and I joined him.

"Did it occur to you that I might not approve of this? That perhaps Fritz is my private chef and of some worth to me, both personally and professionally?"

"Certainly, my dear Jules." He smiled. "That's why I didn't want to discuss any of this with you before sending Charles on his errand. I didn't want to waste the time. You see, there really isn't much choice. I can be very effective here, and I intend to remain. Come. It won't be for long. Enjoy your beer."

I sat and thought in silence. He was right, but it was aggravating. What was I to do with Fritz gone? Suddenly I realized what had begun to nag me.

"I gather, then, that you've cleared Fritz? You might have mentioned it to me."

He did not respond in any way.

"Well?" I said.

He sighed. "There are simply some matters that I can't disclose at this time, even to you, Jules."

"That's ridiculous!"

"Patently, it is not."

"Might I ask why?"

He searched for the least objectionable way to phrase it. "You are a valuable ally, Jules, and becoming a good friend, but there is a certain ingenuousness in your character that I can turn to my advantage. I must ask you to trust me in this."

"I find it highly insulting."

He got up from the desk and crossed over to me, placing his hand on my shoulder. "It is not that, I assure you." He leaned his huge bulk back against the desk. "My father, Jules, had a companion for many years—a very good man of impeccable character and great bravery. But his goodness was so ingrained, his honesty so natural, that he was absolutely incapable of dissembling. My father knew this, of course, and occasionally had to leave this man in the dark, or in a few cases actually mislead him, so that he might not unwittingly tip a winning hand."

Again, his hand came to rest on my shoulder. "Jules, forgive me, but you are not an actor. You are an agent, and a valuable man of action, but if you were closing in on Marcel's murderer, I doubt if you could altogether suppress your feelings until the optimum moment. And that, in this case, is essential."

"But Fritz . . . ?" I began.

"For the time being, let Fritz be my problem. I will say this much: if he is our man, what better place to monitor his activities than under my own roof?"

I was not completely happy or convinced by his rationale, but I could see that his mind was made up. He went back around his desk and sat, and we waited for the others to return. Lupa opened the last beer, poured it for himself, and had nearly finished when Vernet entered.

He was of average height but distinguished by a full red beard and, incongruously, piercing dark eyes. It was an odd combination, which his dress reinforced. He wore an English derby hat and a large plaid overcoat, which, when removed, gave way to more conventional attire—a dark suit and tie.

The color scheme of his face became even more bizarre when he took off the hat, revealing a head of gray hair. He entered by the tunnel, so of course we'd been warned of his entrance.

"See here, Auguste, what's this about closing down the restaurant? I realize that 'M' and Altamont have asked me to cooperate in every way I could, but we're beginning to lose customers, what with Charles's cooking and your irregular hours. What's the explanation this time?"

Perfectly unruffled, Lupa introduced us.

"Now, sit down, monsieur. I am sorry, but it's really un- avoidable. We should be open for business again within the hour, but in the meantime I am going to need your help. Will you have some beer? Cognac?"

The owner sat and nodded. "Courvoisier, *s'il vous plait.*" To my surprise, Lupa attended him. When they had both been seated, Lupa began again.

"We have a real problem, though we could possibly have foreseen it, given the way the police have handled everything so far. They've reached the inescapable conclusion that I am Monsieur Routier's murderer. Monsieur Giraud has just given me that report, and the police are supposedly to be here this evening to arrest me. Unfortunately, that would be most in- convenient, so I've covered over the door to the office and decided to remain here until I've settled this matter. Let it look to the police as if I've run. That's fine; in fact, it suits my purposes, since now the heat will be off the actual mur- derer. They'll of course question you as to my whereabouts, and you should tell them that you dismissed me immediately upon learning that my papers were forged and you haven't seen me since."

"Fine," said Vernet with impatience, pulling at his beard, "but who's to be the new chef? How did I find him? And, above all, can he cook?"

"On the last point, you may rest assured. His name is Fritz Benet, and he would be worthy to be my own chef, were I ever in a position to be able to afford one. Maybe after the war . . . but that's irrelevant. He's been the chef for Monsieur Giraud for quite some time. However, for these purposes Giraud fired him because he suspected him of complicity with Routier's death."

"Now, wait a minute, Auguste . . ." I began, but he waved me down.

"That puts him in no danger. Believe me, it's perfectly safe. The police have checked him thoroughly."

"But why should I suspect him?"

"He poured the beer." He shrugged. "It doesn't have to make sense to us. It merely has to be plausible to the police. They've apparently settled on me. That you might suspect Fritz will have no bearing."

Vernet sipped at his cognac. "So I will once again have a restaurant."

"Barring difficulties."

That seemed to palliate him. His face relaxed and he looked at me. "I asked for this when I decided to accommodate our friend here. At least it's not dull."

Lupa picked up the book he'd been reading when I entered and, without so much as a "by your leave," became engrossed again. Vernet and I discussed Fritz's merits until the alarm sounded again. Lupa distractedly pushed the button, and I, seeing that he was taking no precautions, got up and walked into the tunnel, my pistol ready. After a few moments, I heard Fritz's voice and returned to my chair.

When they entered, Fritz crossed over to me.

"You're all right?" he asked.

"Perfectly."

"What's the trouble?"

Lupa spoke. "Hello, Fritz. Please take a seat."

Within a quarter of an hour, the thing had been settled, and Fritz was in the kitchen, getting acquainted. Vernet waited for the police in the bar upstairs, and Charles, somewhat miffed at his demotion, nevertheless was assisting Fritz whenever necessary. Lupa and I sat in the office, discussing the war.

"I still say that it will be over soon. Now that Italy has joined us . . ."

Lupa shook his head. "Jules, you are deluded. This war will continue for years."

"Years? Don't be ridiculous!"

"Mark my words. You talk of settling down and growing your vineyards in peace. In two years, you'll be wondering if you'll be able to hold on to your land. The government will need every man, every resource, and it will take them. Your hobbies, which you so treasure, and rightly so, will fade to insignificance. There will be no good food available. Everyone will join in the effort. Watkins has brought me the news that they'll soon be hiring women at the munitions factories."

"No!"

"Yes, indeed. Every man will be fighting. Factory workers, sick men, even older men will be forced to the front, and it will be to no avail. The war will drag on. Keep in mind, Jules, it's only been ten months. There's still adventure and idealism in the thought of war. Give the world two or three or five years of it, and you'll see everything you know change. After this case is over, I'm quitting myself, though my uncle will disapprove. I may have to go to America to escape this war, though I fear that even the Americans and their pacifist Wilson will have to join. Luckily for France, they'll support her."

"Not exactly a Utopian, are you?"

"No, a realist. They don't go well together."

Knowing that cynicism and youth were constant companions, I was not unduly depressed by his opinions, though it saddened me to see such an intelligent man obviously unaware of the military realities. Germany was strong, but we'd been beaten in 1871 and had learned from it. The Kaiser was no Bismarck. That was the point to remember. No German army would ever march under the Arch de Triomphe again.

"You French," he continued, "with your *elan vital*! It isn't will that wins a war, it's firepower. This war won't be settled by men being pushed against other men on the fronts but in the countries themselves—where every effort of the economy, the government, the citizenry itself will play a part. And it will be at least two years before that fact is realized. No, Jules. Prepare yourself for a long siege."

"And you," I said, "how will you avoid conscription?"

He sat back. "I am willing to die, I suppose, for freedom, and I am more than willing to devote my talents to serve the

Allied cause. But I could never, ever serve on the front as one of the thousands who are important because they are bodies. My ego would never permit it. And honestly, Jules, would yours?"

I looked down at my hands. "I'd rather not serve at the front, if that's what you mean, but in my case it's more a question of age than conceit."

He shrugged. "Call it what you will. Are you getting ready to go?"

I'd gotten up, alerted by noises upstairs. He put his fingers to his lips as he crossed over to me, and together we listened at the door to what sounded like Magiot himself talking to Vernet.

"You expect me to believe that he left here this afternoon and left no hint of where he was going?"

"I expect nothing, monsieur," Vernet replied. "I merely tell you what happened. I dismissed him. He left. *C'est ça. C'est tout.*"

Magiot asked a couple of questions about Fritz and then, angry but satisfied with the responses, left. So it had worked.

Lupa walked back to his chair and sat. "Satisfactory. Jules, you're going home this evening? Good. Would you check something for me?"

"Of course."

"The table in your sitting room, in front of the fireplace, I'd like you to look at it carefully and describe it to me in detail when you return tomorrow."

I left him exactly as I'd found him, sitting over a book at

his desk. I found my way out easily through the tunnel, walked to the car, and began the drive home. It had been a long day. Only as I turned off the light near my bed to sleep did I remember that the telegram from Georges hadn't arrived.

· 14 ·

Tuesday, May 25, 1915. The day broke cool and clear. I
threw the comforter off and got to my feet. Downstairs, the kitchen was spotless as always but, without Fritz,
seemed lifeless. I made my own coffee, which was not good,
and ate one of yesterday's croissants, which was worse. I
hadn't seen Tania since Sunday after the shooting, and so I
decided to pay her a call.

The walk to her house was always pleasant for me, and no
less so this morning. The greens were vibrant, and I'd gotten
started early enough to hear the birds chirping. It was not
quite cold, though I walked with my hands in my pockets.

Danielle answered my knock and stood wringing her hands
in the doorway.

"Is madame in?" I inquired.

She shook her head back and forth and looked at me
helplessly.

"What's the matter, Danielle?"

I brushed past her and on into the foyer. "Tania!" There was no answer.

"Elle est partie." Danielle had come up behind me.

"Where's she gone to? When did she leave?"

The domestic only shook her head, tears coming to her eyes.

"The other woman? What about her?"

"She's also gone."

"When did they leave? Have you no idea?"

"They were gone when I got up this morning. They were here last night. Oh, Monsieur Giraud, I'm so worried. I don't know what could have happened. Everything was normal last night, and now they are gone. There is no note. I heard nothing."

She was becoming hysterical, so I walked her to a chair and we sat down. I took her hand.

"Now look, Danielle. Try to remember. Did anyone come last night? Did madame act strange in any way? How was the other woman?"

"Last night she was walking around, of course with the bandage still on her head. But we talked, and she seemed well. The madame had dinner and went up to bed early, complaining of a headache. No one came to the house."

"What time did you get up this morning?"

"At dawn, monsieur, *comme d'habitude*."

"Were there any signs of trouble? Struggle of any kind?"

"No."

"All right. Wait here. I'll look around."

So saying, I left her in the sitting room and went to Tania's room. The bed had been slept in. Her cosmetics were neatly arranged. Her brush had some hair in it—since Danielle cleaned daily, it was likely that Tania had taken the time to comb out her hair. Everything was in order.

On Tania's bureau there was a framed photograph of herself, her husband, and the four boys formally posed around their sitting room mantel. The focus was clear, all the likenesses visible. From the age of the boys, the picture had been taken within the past two years. I remembered Lupa's directions and my hand reached out to take the thing. But then I stopped. Could I do this to my lover? Were there no limits to this intelligence gathering? How would Tania react to the missing picture? Turning abruptly, I left the room empty-handed.

In the other rooms, I looked at windows for signs of forcible entry, for scuff marks in the hall which might show where a struggle had taken place, but I found nothing. Anna's bandage lay in a wastebasket near her dressing table, but she may have had it changed. I came back down to find Danielle as I'd left her, but now dabbing at her eyes more frequently. The girl was not yet twenty and no doubt was easily upset.

"There, there," I said, which was patently no help. She cried for another small time before I could quiet her by suggesting that she go to my house, until further notice, and try to keep the place in order. Even as I said it, I cursed to myself. I'd forgotten to look over the table near the hearth. Still, it was no great matter. I was worried about Tania's disappearance. If nothing else, it was badly timed. What would Lupa say when he heard that Anna had disappeared? I didn't care to think about it.

As we were about to lock up the house, I excused myself for a moment, trudging wearily back up the stairs to Tania's room. Carefully I removed the family portrait from the frame, rolled it, and placed it in my coat pocket. If it would serve to clear her of suspicion, she would have to do without it for a time. On the way back down the stairs, I tried to rationalize my guilt by telling myself that, had she been there, I would have asked to borrow the picture, and she would have acceded. It was small consolation.

We carefully locked up the house and walked together as far as the road. I was in a hurry to get to Valence, though I couldn't have said why—perhaps I was as much concerned with getting out of Danielle's presence. Nothing upset me more than the whimpering voice of an hysterical teenager. Be that as it may, I left her with my keys and turned to Valence. I found myself breathing hard and forced myself to a slow walk. It would be good if, as Lupa said, this thing was coming to a head. I was afraid I wouldn't be able to stand the pace much longer.

I stopped at the first cafe *en ville* and ordered a double espresso and a newspaper. By the time I'd finished both, it was close to nine o'clock and traffic had picked up on the road. I felt much more relaxed and decided for the moment to put off seeing Lupa. Shut up as he was in his hideaway at La Couronne, he would not be of much help in determining Tania's and Anna's whereabouts anyway. And I was still not at all sure that the ladies were at risk. Walking out of the cafe, I glanced in the direction of St. Etienne and saw sulfur clouds beginning to rise. So the factory was still producing. Things hadn't gotten out of control yet.

I headed toward the telegraph office to check on early telegrams. Perhaps they hadn't bothered to deliver Georges's telegram of the night before, or maybe it had only arrived this morning. No such luck. Nothing had arrived for me at all.

Again out on the street, I turned toward the police station, thinking it would seem logical to Magiot if I showed an interest in whether they'd taken Lupa or not. The way my morning had been going, Magiot might even cheer me up.

I was ushered directly into his office. He rose to greet me, and we shook hands.

"Well, Jules, what wakes you so early?"

I'd play his game. "Curiousity, Jacques. I wanted to see if eight o'clock came twice a day. Someone told me it appeared in the morning, and I wanted to check it out for myself."

He smiled tolerantly.

"But," I said, "I really thought I'd drop by and see if you'd picked up Lupa or gotten anywhere with this thing. I had a devil of a time sleeping last night, what with all your talk of international affairs. Have you got him? Did he confess?"

Magiot arranged some papers on his desk, taking his time. He got out a cigarette, offered me one which I refused, and lit it. "No," he said finally, "we didn't get him. He'd left La Couronne by the time we'd come to arrest him."

"Lupa left? When did he go? I saw him there only yesterday morning."

"Evidently Vernet fired him outright when he learned of the forged papers. He packed up and left immediately. You know they've hired your man—Fritz, isn't it?—to take his place?"

"No. No, I didn't know that."

"By the way, Jules, why did you fire him just at this time?"

I shrugged. "I found myself not trusting him. It wasn't

anything specific that brought it on, but since he'd brought in the beers that night, it occurred to me that he'd had as good a chance as anyone to poison one of them. I kept getting more and more nervous as mealtimes approached, until finally I wasn't enjoying his cooking, so I let him go."

"But I understand he brought the beers in on a tray from which everyone selected . . ."

"True. As I said, it wasn't anything specific. I just can't have a man in my house whom I don't trust completely. He could have arranged it, possibly."

"Yes, from your point of view, possible. I think you've been unjust, though it's your right."

I shrugged again. "There are other chefs. But what are you doing about Lupa? Have you any ideas?"

"None, really. He didn't leave by train. At least, no one saw him leave by train. He could really be anywhere. We've wired all the neighboring towns and asked for their hotel lists, though of course he'll change his name. He may have sheafs of forged papers. Still, I think we'll get him. You can rest assured."

"I hope so. Why, though, did you wait until last night to go for him? Surely you could have picked him up at any time."

"We'd already been by in the morning, if you remember what I told you yesterday—it must have been after you had talked to him, because he wasn't there. We reasoned our best chance to find him was during dinner hours. With the force so shorthanded we couldn't leave someone there to cover the doors at all times, so we gambled and lost."

"A shame," I said, sincerely.

"Damned right," he agreed, stubbing out his cigarette. "And now, old friend, if there's nothing else, I should be getting on to routines. I'm glad to see you showing some interest at least. Do drop around later if you have any more questions. We should have him within the week."

"Yes. Well, thank you for your time, Jacques. I know the way out."

Out in the corridor, I allowed myself a smile. Passing through the lobby, my hands in my pockets and my head down, I heard a familiar voice. The American accent echoed unmelodically off the marble walls. I stopped and saw Paul leaning over the reception desk, obviously angry.

"But I've been reporting at St. Etienne every day for a week now! I can't be there tonight. Don't you understand? I can report here just as well . . ."

The gendarme replied in a low voice.

"Well, all right then, arrest me, but at least let me . . ."

I tapped him on the shoulder. "Paul," I said.

He stopped and turned. "Jules, thank God. Listen, can you help me? These people don't seem to realize that I can't report to St. Etienne this evening."

"Why not?"

"I received a wire from my publishers telling me to meet their representative tonight in Valence. So I thought it would be a simple enough matter to report here, but this man here keeps telling me that it's against the rules. If I were told to report in St. Etienne, then I must report in St. Etienne. It's insane. What's the goddam difference?"

"Why don't you just wire the representative to meet you in St. Etienne?"

"He's already left by now, Jules. If I'm not here, they won't take it lightly."

"I imagine not. All right, let me talk to him."

I leaned over the desk and pointed out to the *flic* that since they already had a suspect, it was rather pointless to keep hounding everyone else involved. Perhaps Monsieur Magiot would see the logic of my position. At the mention of the chief's name, the desk guard looked down and mumbled that perhaps something could be done to accommodate the monsieur. I told him I sincerely hoped so. Then I turned, took Paul's arm, and walked out the front door.

Out on the stoop, I put my arm around him. "Well, how are you?"

"Fine, now, thank you. Let me buy you a drink."

"*Volontiers.*"

We settled in a cafe, and I surprised both Paul and myself by ordering a Vichy water.

"What were you doing in the station?" he asked. "I certainly didn't expect to run into you there."

"Oh, the police chief here is an old acquaintance of mine. Yesterday he told me they were going to arrest Lupa, and—"

"So it was him. I'm damned."

"Not necessarily. The police have decided it was him, and he's left town—"

"Well, that clinches it."

"Well, yes, it appears so. Anyway, I was at the station to see if they'd got him and found all this out. Seems his papers were forged, too."

He sipped at his whiskey. "Doesn't surprise me any, though."

"No?"

"No. Look at it like this, Jules. We'd all been meeting there at your place for a long time, and if anybody wanted to kill Marcel they could have done it any old time. But everybody liked Marcel. 'Course there's other reasons for killing than having it be personal. But anyway, this Lupa fellow comes in, and right off Marcel is killed, and then Lupa runs away. Didn't he have to register every day? He was foreign, too, wasn't he?"

"I suppose they asked him to. But no, since he was in town, they only requested that he not leave."

"Well, there, now. I hope they hang the bastard."

We were sitting on the sidewalk, and the talk turned to other matters. It was a fine day, and we chatted until noon and then decided to have a bite.

Halfway through our ham sandwiches, Paul looked up across the street and spoke. "It's old home week at Grand Central." He motioned with his head to a couple walking toward us on the other side of the road, as yet unaware of us. It was Georges and Madame Pulis. When they were abreast of us, Paul called out to them.

"The secret's out now about you two. Come on over and join us and maybe we won't tell Henri."

They stopped abruptly, waved, and waited for the traffic to let up. Georges took her by the arm and, limping nimbly, guided her to our table. They ordered drinks, and while waiting for them to arrive, Georges continued the teasing.

"Now that it's known, my dear, why hide it any longer?"

He winked at us as Madame Pulis flushed crimson. Taking her hand, he gave it a gallant kiss. "Or is it to be *au revoir?*" He turned his head away in mock despair.

"Oh, Georges, stop." Madame Pulis was rather heavily set, but not unattractive when she wasn't crying. She smiled broadly and took us all in. "Georges came by to see Henri, but he's off delivering somewhere, so Georges offered to accompany me to the market. That's all there is to it."

"What's the line about the lady protesting too much?" asked Georges, laughing.

She blushed again as the drinks arrived.

"What brings you back so early, Georges?" I asked. "I thought you weren't due in Valence until tomorrow evening."

"Luck," he said. "Two appointments canceled. Just as well. I could use the time off."

"You've heard the news, haven't you?" Paul piped in.

"What's that?"

"Last night the police went to arrest Lupa for Marcel's death, and he'd left town."

Georges sipped at his Pernod. "So, it wasn't one of us. I'm relieved."

"You didn't really think it was?" Madame Pulis asked.

He shrugged. "No one really knew too much about anyone else in our group. When I heard the rumors about the espionage angle, I must admit I became concerned. I didn't suspect anyone, but then I couldn't completely trust anyone either. Now it's a relief."

"It will make tomorrow night much more pleasant," I said. "By the way, it's going to be at La Couronne, where Lupa worked, coincidentally. None of you mind, do you?"

"Not at all," Paul replied. "At least, I don't. Anybody else?"

Georges spoke up. "*Moi non plus.* But why there?"

"Because the owner there, Monsieur Vernet, is a friend of mine, and I've loaned him Fritz until he has time to find another chef." I didn't see any harm in telling them a different story from the one I'd told Magiot. "In return for which I eat there gratis myself. Believe me, I'd never have let Fritz go if it would have meant eating my own cuisine, if you could call it that."

Paul called for the waiter and ordered another round of drinks, and Madame Pulis said she really had to be getting on to the market.

"Shall I join you?" asked Georges.

"Thank you, no. I'm perfectly happy to go alone. Good day, gentlemen."

"A charming creature," said Georges after she'd gone.

"What's she going to the market for? Doesn't Henri own a store?" Paul was relaxing with his third *demi.*

Georges shrugged. "The company, I suppose."

"I hope we didn't embarrass her too much," I said. "She doesn't seem to enjoy that kind of humor."

"Oh, she's fine. Henri and I tease her like that all the time. She just doesn't know you two so well." He paused. "I'm afraid I have a bit of sad news, however. This will be my last Wednesday beer party. I've been transferred to Algiers."

Paul put down his beer. "Well, as you fellows would say, *merde!*"

"You echo my sentiments, but there's nothing I can do about it other than quit, which I can't afford. It's going to be hard. I've come to like this place very much. Not to mention *mes amis.*" He lifted his glass to us.

"When are you going?"

"The ship sails from Marseilles on Sunday, so I thought I'd take the train on Thursday or Friday, probably Friday. I'll have some packing."

"It's lucky the police have decided on Lupa," I said. "Otherwise you might have a problem leaving here."

"Yes," he said, "now that you mention it, it is fortunate. I didn't mention this matter to the company, of course. They'd probably object to one of their salesmen being suspected of murder." He smiled feebly. "Well, at least it's over."

"Not really," put in Paul. "They haven't got him yet, and until they do, I'm not going to rest easy. You don't know it, Georges, but he also killed a police inspector last week."

"Have they proved that, too?"

"Yep. Strangled him right on the road."

"Mon dieu!"

I decided to join in. "I feel I must apologize for inviting him. Possibly all this could have been avoided if . . ."

"Oh, nonsense, Jules. How could you have known? If Lupa were a spy of some sort—mind you, I'm not saying he was, but if he was—there'd be no way any of us could have known. Don't blame yourself. All of us only got to know you, and each other as well for that matter, because of your nature, because you trust the people you like."

"Exactly," Paul said, "like we were sayin' yesterday."

"But do they have any evidence that Lupa *was* a spy?" Georges asked.

"Either no, or they won't say. You've got to know this

man, Magiot, the police chief, to appreciate him. They don't, at least from my talks with him, have any case to speak of against Lupa. Of course, his running won't help him any. They certainly don't have a motive, except this nebulous espionage thing. Magiot needs to solve this murder, and he will, even if he has to get the wrong man."

"So you don't think it was Lupa?" asked Paul.

"I just don't know."

"Then who do you think it was? One of us?"

"No. I really don't think that. It was undoubtedly Lupa, but Magiot's case on him is so weak that to try and prove anything by it would be folly."

"Except that he ran," offered Georges.

"Except that he ran," I agreed.

"And it might be that Magiot just didn't tell you everything he knows, *n'est-ce pas?*"

I also agreed with that.

Having finished his beer, Paul stood up. "Well, I must be going along. Try to get some sleep before my meeting tonight. You say Fritz is cooking at La Couronne? Maybe I'll meet my publisher's representative there."

"You're not going back to St. Etienne?"

"No, no. I took a hotel room in town for today."

Georges and I thanked Paul for the drinks. I'd stuck with Vichy throughout and felt good. Paul was a bit tipsy, and Georges offered to walk him to his hotel. They left, saying they'd see me the following night.

I got up and began walking toward Anna's flower shop. Too many things were happening too quickly, and I was becoming very worried about the two women. It was comforting to agree with the others talking about the solution to the murders, but of course Lupa hadn't done it. One of my friends had. I felt for my pistol, tucked close under my armpit. I was glad I hadn't been drinking.

It was not yet late afternoon, and I still didn't feel like seeing Lupa, so I walked aimlessly past the flower shop. No one was inside. I strolled on through the town, past a group of training soldiers in their red pants and blue tunics, out to where the buildings grew more sparse and the fields began. Under a large oak that was beginning to bud, I sat and thought of Tania.

She had gone, left me without a note or a word, and I could put off the inevitable thought no longer. It was beginning to look as if Lupa had grounds for his suspicions. It was entirely possible that Tania had used me, used Ponty, used even her husband before us. And now she had disappeared, along with the secrets that she had said we never kept from one another. I understood then the real reason I hadn't rushed to consult Lupa—I could barely stand to confront myself with my gullibility. Lupa's reaction to the disappearance, whether it was scorn or compassion, would be unbearable.

A great world-weariness came and settled over me. I leaned back against the tree, defeated, and closed my eyes.

The sun was setting when I awoke with a start. Something from a dream had bothered me, and realizing what it had been, I woke up. It had been a clear day when I'd begun to doze, and looking in the direction of St. Etienne, I should have seen the familiar pillars of sulfur smoke rising over the city.

There had been none.

· 15 ·

Though I moved quickly, the walk back to Anna's shop seemed interminable. Dusk had settled over the town completely by now, making the unfamiliar section of town even more so. Once again the door was locked, and I quietly slipped the lock and stepped inside. This time I let the alarm sound, though of course I couldn't hear it.

Lupa was behind his desk again. He was, as usual, dressed in brown and yellow. It was as though he hadn't moved since the last time I had seen him, except now that he expected me, he was looking at the entrance to the tunnel as I entered his office.

"Getting pretty sure of yourself, aren't you?" I said. "Suppose that hadn't been me?"

He smiled. "Then I should have had to shoot you." So saying, he lifted his hand above the level of the desk. It held his pistol. "Thank you, though, for the warning. I appreciate it."

With what seemed a great effort, he pushed back the chair and, standing, reached out his hand. It was, I realized, our first handshake. "Where have you been? I was beginning to get worried."

"I wanted some time for myself," I said, "and I ran into most of our suspects."

"Indeed?"

"Paul and Georges. We had a fine time. They'll both be coming tomorrow night. But I have news."

He was sitting again. "So have I. Will you have a beer?"

He reached up to his left and pulled a cord which had been newly strung along the ceiling. Two quick pulls. I looked at him questioningly.

"For Fritz," he explained. "We've worked out a code so that I don't starve or die of thirst. Two pulls for beer. If anyone else is about, he unlatches the bell."

As he finished speaking, the door opened and Fritz entered with a tray. Seeing me, he smiled. "Hello, sir. Good to see you."

Lupa spoke. "Fritz, Monsieur Giraud would also like some beer, and he'll be dining with us. You will, won't you?"

"Of course."

When Fritz had brought the other beer and gone, Lupa poured for both of us, waited for the foam to settle in his glass, took a large gulp, then looked at me. "Well?"

"There's no smoke rising over St. Etienne."

He sat immobile, his face showing nothing. With his left hand, he drummed his fingertips on the desktop. He sighed deeply.

"So. In that case, we can do nothing about it. Watkins

should be here before long with a report. Did you check the table?"

"No. I forgot."

He drank. "Hmm . . . well, I have news."

"So you said."

"I've gotten through to my uncle about your retirement, and he's persuaded your people to accept your decision, though if you were younger . . ."

I nodded. "You needn't say it." If I were younger, I wouldn't have to worry very much about my future, it would be very short.

"You said you met Paul and Georges today. I had understood that Georges wouldn't be back until tomorrow. And what is Paul doing in Valence?"

I reported on my day from the time I reached the police station. He listened without moving, leaning back in his chair with his eyes closed. He might have been asleep. When I'd finished, he opened his eyes and, seeing his glass empty, poured another beer.

"So they're all happy to believe me the culprit. Understandable, I suppose. Anything else?"

"Well," I hesitated, "yes, actually. Tania and Anna are missing."

He then did something I never thought I'd witness. His glass was on its way to his mouth when I spoke, and he arrested it midway and set it back on the desk.

"When did you find this out?"

"This morning."

"Why didn't you report it immediately?"

"What could you have done? You're effectively a prisoner

here." I began defensively, angry at myself for not having come by sooner, for allowing myself to be lulled by my smaller duties, my social obligations. After I had run into Paul and then Georges, I'd felt as though I might stumble upon some solution. Twice I'd headed to La Couronne to see Lupa, and twice I'd decided against it. My suffering self-esteem had needed—stupidly, I now realized—to present him with answers, not questions. I had wrongly persisted in viewing Tania's (and Anna's) disappearance as my own problem, not our common problem.

"I'm sorry," I said. "I retract that."

"No need to," he said. "It's close to the truth."

"No, I should have come immediately. If anything has happened to them . . ."

A trace of humanity appeared in the hard eyes. He, too, knew both sides—the concern and the suspicion. "Tell me about it now," he said, "and we'll try to make up for the lost time."

I filled him in on my search of Tania's house, how there appeared to have been no struggle. The only inexplicable thing was their failure to tell Danielle.

"Don't you consider that strange?"

"Yes, rather."

"Everything else was in order?"

"Perfectly. Oh, and one other thing."

I took out the photograph and handed it to him. He unrolled it and placed it flat on the top of his desk, staring at it intently. "Yes," he said absently, "satisfactory. Just as I suspected." So saying, he rerolled the picture and placed it in his desk drawer.

"What?"

"In good time, Jules. In good time."

He ruminated for a while. Finally, he straightened in his chair, reaching for the nearly forgotten beer. He drank it off in a gulp. "Well, they *are* women, given to all sorts of odd whims, and there's nothing to be done at this time. Let's see if they return this evening. If not . . ."

He was interrupted by the alarm. He reached for the switch and turned off the sound, and this time got up to check the tunnel himself. "That should be Watkins," he said. "Would you ring for more beer?"

While I did so, he disappeared. Fritz entered almost immediately, the tray laden this time.

"How do you like it here?" I asked.

He shrugged. "It reminds me of my apprenticeship. The orders are too large, and I spend too much time catering to uneducated palates. Of course, I'm excluding Monsieur Lupa's. I hope this situation won't last for too long. What have you eaten today?"

I told him, and he shuddered. "I could arrange to have Charles deliver fresh croissants, and as for coffee . . ."

"Really, Fritz, that won't be necessary. I'll survive, though I also hope this charade doesn't go on much longer. I suppose you should know that Danielle is now watching over the house."

"A woman in my kitchen? You'll have to watch her, sir. Don't let her use any of—"

I raised a palm. "It's all right, Fritz. I'll try to keep her under control."

One of the conditions I'd met in hiring Fritz was a guar-
antee that I wouldn't let a woman meddle in his affairs in the
kitchen, but this seemed to be a special case. "She'll be gone
by the time you return."

Lupa returned with Watkins and told Fritz that we'd now
have three for dinner. Watkins looked the same as when I'd
first met him, complete with swollen cheek, except that he
was dirtier. There were smudges on his clothes and face. Lupa
dismissed Fritz and he left.

"Suppose someone sees him going out?" I asked.

He looked at me with impatience. "He locks the outside
door before coming in. Ah, more beer." He sat, and bade us
do likewise. After we were settled, he turned to Watkins.
"Well?"

He emptied the olive pits into his hand, then dumped
them into the wastebasket next to the desk. "It's blown."

"Yes. We know. Report."

He looked at us, surprised. "But how could you know?"

"There was no smoke," I replied.

"But that's the funny thing. The stacks stopped smoking
nearly an hour before the explosion. I thought at the time—"

"Enough!" Lupa bellowed. "Begin at the beginning."

"Yes, sir. This morning I got up at dawn, as usual, and
when I got to my post, there was already activity around the
factory. Evidently today there was a big shipment scheduled.
By the way, last night I was followed again, at least back to
my hotel."

"Same man?" Lupa asked.

"Yes, sir. I'm sure of it."

"Did you get a better look at his face this time?"

"Yes, sir. I think I could identify him."

"Satisfactory. Go on."

"So I stayed my ground until nine o'clock or thereabouts, and a chilly ground it was, though not so bad as yesterday. Anyway, then I made it out to the road to Valence and waited for Pulis. He showed up in about an hour by horsecart, loaded with supplies. I kind of expected him to dawdle around, but he rode directly to the loading gate and left the cart with the guards while he crossed the street and had some coffee."

"He never went inside the gate?"

"No. They don't allow it."

"How long did the unloading take?"

"No more than a quarter hour. Then they sent a man over to get him, and he picked up the cart and started back out of town. I followed him back to where I'd picked him up, but he looked like he was just heading back here, so I let him go. I didn't like leaving the factory unwatched for so long. Then I got back and watched them arranging things for shipment for a time. Old Ponty kept running in and out, wiping his forehead and giving directions, but otherwise nothing happened for the next hour. Then, around noon, a woman came to the gate, and I recognized her as the one you, uh, you've been seeing."

"Tania was there?" I asked.

He nodded.

"Was she alone?"

"She came alone and went inside. Then, a few minutes later, she left with Ponty. They were gone maybe an hour for lunch, or I suppose it was lunch."

"How were they acting?" put in Lupa.

"I couldn't say, sir, I was too far away."

"All right. Continue."

"They returned at about one, as I said, and both went back inside. After only a few minutes, she came back out and left. I was tempted to follow her, but you'd only said to follow Pulis if it looked promising, so I stayed. I'm glad I did. For about an hour, it was the same story of loading and unloading, with Ponty running around again—and then, all of a sudden, the stacks stopped smoking, as I said. Everyone was so busy I doubt if they even noticed. No matter. I stayed put and waited."

"Good," Lupa said. "Did anyone enter or leave after Madame Chessal?"

"Yes, the janitor."

"When did he go?"

"Maybe ten minutes after the smoking stopped."

"Is that his normal quitting time?"

"I can't say for sure, sir. The other times I've been there, he's left at all different times. Last night he was evidently still on duty when I left, and that was late. Maybe his schedule varies on different days."

"All right." Lupa nodded, and Watkins continued.

"About three o'clock, then, Ponty came out to check on something at the guard's gate. Some of the trucks had started their motors, and things appeared to be getting under way, when all of a sudden the whole place just blew up from inside. It was something to see."

"I'd imagine so."

"When things settled a bit, I ran over, as if I were a bystander, to see if I could help. The whole building had been leveled, but outside, things weren't so bad, not so bad as I'd imagined from the size of the explosion." He reached into his pocket—"Anyone care for an olive?"—and continued. "Ponty was already up and around, trying to help wherever he could, and he did get a few of the trucks on the road, but generally he was running around in circles, and I can't say that I blame him. There were an awful lot of dead and hurt, so I moved back so as not to be in anybody's way. Before too long, the troops came and cordoned off the area, but I got friendly with one of them and found out that they thought it was the ammunition room that had blown. So I came here."

"Satisfactory," Lupa said. "You did well." He turned to me. "You told me that the ammunition room was impossible to enter."

"It seemed to be."

"Hmm . . ." He leaned back and closed his eyes. Watkins and I watched him thinking for nearly a minute, though it seemed much longer. Finally, he sighed and sat up.

"Yes," he said. "No doubt of it."

There was a knock at the office door, and I got up to open it. It was Fritz, announcing dinner.

We cleared the desk to make room for the dishes. Fritz brought in a bowl so that Watkins could wash himself, and then began bringing in the courses. Being in danger didn't seem to have any effect on Lupa's appetite. I hardly touched the oyster bisque, and though the shad roe was superb, even for Fritz, I found it difficult to get it down. Lupa, on the other hand, ate with relish, talking animatedly about the new book he was reading, the socialist Jaure's *L'Armee Nouvelle*. I tried to steer the conversation back around to the explosion, but he insisted we leave it until we'd dined.

"Business during meals upsets the digestion. In this case especially, there is nothing more to discuss." He continued unperturbed through the crème caramel and coffee, while Watkins and I glanced at each other from time to time, shaking our heads.

He rang for Fritz to come clear the service, but there was no response. Evidently someone else was in the kitchen, and he'd unlatched the bell.

Lupa moved everything to one side, poured himself another cup of coffee, and sat back in his chair. I lit a cigarette and stared at him.

"Yes?" he said finally.

"I was casually wondering what we should do now."

"You're sure that everyone will be here tomorrow?"

I nodded and he sighed contentedly.

"Then there's nothing else to be done. You may as well go on home. This affair will conclude tomorrow night. Indeed, it is over now—there only remains to wrap it up and deliver it to your friend Magiot."

I thought he was kidding me. "Oh, fine," I said. "Should I call him now?"

"I think not. It would be premature. Tomorrow will suffice. I'll take care of it."

I humored him. "Why do you want Magiot here at all?"

He sipped at his coffee. "So that he'll be convinced not to harass me." He tried the bell again. "Now, I suggest that tomorrow you see no one until you arrive here, and of course mention to no one that I'll be present. Our man no doubt thinks the heat is off. It would be instructive to watch him react when he discovers he's wrong."

"Yes," I said, "and, just for the record, who should we be watching?"

He looked shocked. "Is it possible you don't know? I'm sure it will be clear if you reflect on it. Ah, Fritz, excellent! You were right about the cognac in the bisque—far more delicate than the sherry. I salute you."

Fritz, who had just entered with his apron, bowed. *"Merci."*

"Who was in the kitchen just now?" Lupa asked.

"Monsieur Anser. He wanted to see where the meeting would be held tomorrow night, so I showed him my quarters. He's dining upstairs."

"He's not alone, is he?" I asked.

"I believe so, sir. Should I check again?"

"That won't be necessary," said Lupa. He looked at me. "It makes no difference. As I've said, there's nothing more to be done."

When Fritz had finished clearing, I stood to go. "Have you any ideas about the ladies?"

"Yes. I have an idea that they are in no danger. I would not be surprised if they were back in Madame Chessal's home this very minute."

"Well, then, *à demain.*"

Not much mollified, I turned to go. Watkins held the tapestry aside for me. As I walked through the tunnel, I tried to think of what I had missed that made everything so obvious to Lupa, but to no avail.

I skirted the entrance to La Couronne on the way back,

since Lupa had asked that I avoid the principals. The road was very dark, and it was beginning to get brisk again, so I walked quickly and was abreast of Tania's house in under a quarter of an hour. It was still, to all appearances, closed up. Stopping to light a cigarette, I decided, principal or not, I wanted to see Tania, and so I walked up the drive to the front door.

It was still locked. I pushed the button by the door and set off a chorus of chimes. No lights, no sounds. I rang once more to the same effect, then shrugged and went back to the road. Lupa had been wrong there, and if he were wrong once, he could be again. The night seemed to get chillier.

The light was on in the sitting room of my own house, and I entered to find Danielle sitting on the settee by the front window. She smiled weakly when I entered.

"Evening, sir." She stood, looking much calmer than she had been in the morning. "Have you heard from the madame?"

"Not directly," I said, "but one of my friends saw her to-day in St. Etienne, so she's probably on her way back now." I wished I could have believed what I was saying, but it would do no good to upset the child. "I'm sure she'll be home by tomorrow evening and wondering where you are."

She brought her hands to her face. "Oh, sir. Then I must be off. The madame would be very upset to find me gone."

"It's all right, dear, I'll take care of it. She wasn't there yet when I passed just a few minutes ago. She'll be all right without you for one night."

"You're sure, sir?"

I smiled. If I could do without Fritz . . . "Yes, yes, I'm sure. But for now, have you eaten?"

"No, sir."

"Well, come, that won't do." I led her into the kitchen and found some eggs, cheese, and a few dried mushrooms. Remembering my promise to Fritz, I decided to cook her dinner myself, though it scandalized her.

"What would people say?" she asked. "Monsieur Giraud cooking my dinner?"

I laughed. "What *would* people say now? Just sit down and relax. Would you care for some cognac?"

"Oh no, sir, I couldn't."

"*Au contraire,* you could. I wish you'd join me."

While the omelette was setting, I went and poured us two snifters. She took a sip and made a face. "I usually have spirits with water."

I turned the omelette. "Not tonight," I said. I wanted her to go off to sleep. She ate slowly and carefully. I don't think she tasted a thing.

When she finished, she was drowsy, and I sent her up to my bed. Fritz would never approve of letting a woman into his room alone. I took down a comforter Tania had made for me, turned out the lights, and lay down on the settee to sleep.

Just before I dozed off I became wide-awake, and swore. After getting up and lighting a candle, I walked over to the table by the hearth. I set the candle down and looked carefully. The only mark was the small depression that the detective had noted the previous Wednesday.

"Sir?"

I started. Danielle stood wrapped in a blanket in the foyer.

"I heard you moving. Are you all right?"

"Perfectly," I said. "I'd just forgotten something."

She remained, awkwardly shifting from foot to foot.

"What's the matter?" I asked. "Can't you go to sleep? Would you like some more cognac?"

"No sir, only . . ." she stammered.

"What's wrong, child? Speak up!"

"Well, sir, I just don't know why she wouldn't have left me a note." She started to sob, then turned and ran up the stairs. I went back to the divan and pulled up the comforter.

Neither do I, I thought. Neither do I.

· 16 ·

The next day I awoke early, had coffee alone in the arbor, then worked in the garden, weeding. At noon, I sent Danielle over to Tania's to see if she'd returned, but she hadn't. It was quite warm. At about two o'clock we took a sparse lunch of tomatoes, pâté, and bread, after which I napped while she did some laundry. Finally, when the sun had just set, she helped me load three cases of beer into the Ford, and I drove to La Couronne.

I entered via the front door and asked Charles if he'd help me unload my cargo. A few of the patrons looked up as we passed. It was certainly irregular to make deliveries through the dining room, but no one complained. I was evidently the first to arrive.

Lupa's quarters had been rearranged to accommodate a crowd, with chairs brought down from above and set around the walls. Fritz was busy with dinners, and I watched him for a short time until I became restless and moved back to the apartment for a beer. Generally I waited until some of the group arrived before I drank, but tonight I made an exception.

The next to appear were Georges and Henri—together, as they usually were. Henri was more relaxed than I'd seen him in the past week. We shook hands, and his grip was dry and firm.

"Georges tells me they've arrested Lupa."

"I think not yet," I said.

"But he did it."

"It appears so."

He breathed out. "That's a relief. I was sure they were going to arrest me because I was a foreigner—but then I forgot"—he smiled—"so are Lupa and Paul."

Georges walked up and laid his arm across Henri's shoulders. "I kept telling him last week not to worry. If he'd escaped the arrests last August, the authorities didn't suspect him at all." Georges was referring to the *Carnet B* arrests of suspected foreign agents, which took place upon mobilization. "The same went for Paul, but Lupa—aren't I right, Jules?—came to Valence after August."

I nodded. "That's so. Why don't you have a beer, Henri? And you, too, Georges? I'm sure it's been a hard week for all of us."

We sat, and they began to drink. Henri wiped the foam from his drooping mustache, letting only a few drops fall onto his old faded frock. Georges was dapper in a blue suit and tie. He drank neatly.

"Did Paul make it to the hotel yesterday?" I asked only to make conversation.

"Oh yes." Georges smiled. "Tipsy but in fine spirits. Speaking of which . . ."

Outside, there was a slight hubbub, and in a moment, Paul entered, beaming. "A fine howdy-do this is!" he said. "Starting without me again." He said his hellos all around and picked up a beer. "Good news, friends, my book is sold! Here's to poetry!"

We drank the toast. He turned to me. "They took the new poems. Isn't that great?"

We agreed it was, and he insisted we all open more beer. In the middle of passing them out, he stopped. "Hey, where's the lady?"

I had been worrying about Tania since I'd arrived but was still hoping she would appear. "I don't know," I said, "but I'm sure she'll be around."

We pulled our chairs into a small circle and began to talk about Paul's good fortune. No one seemed disposed to discuss Marcel's death, and since I had no idea of Lupa's intentions, I decided to wait. Finally, there was a knock on the doorjamb, and I turned to see Tania.

"Am I late?" she asked sweetly.

I walked over and embraced her. "Where have you been? I've been worried sick."

She didn't get a chance to answer me, because the other men had come over and bombarded her with their stories of Lupa's guilt and Paul's publishing. So I went and opened a beer for her while she removed her coat and made herself comfortable. When the din had subsided somewhat, she offered her own tidbit: "I've just come from St. Etienne."

The news, of course, had been in the paper that day, and

I'd been a bit surprised that no one had brought it up before, but each had had his own personal matters, which were of some importance.

She continued. "That's why I was late, and I'm sorry, but there was much to do. I'd gone yesterday to have lunch with Maurice—he's so lonely, I feel I owe him at least that, Jules—and afterward, planned to go shopping with a friend. It was horrible, really horrible. I'd like that beer, please." I handed it to her.

"Do you know what happened?" asked Henri. "I was there yesterday morning."

"Only what you've read, I presume. The ammunition room blew up. The guards were killed instantly, so they don't know whether someone succeeded in getting in."

"Grisly," said Georges.

"Very," she agreed. "I should have been back last night," she said to me, "but I stayed behind to help with the nursing."

Fritz came to the door, knocked, and entered, closing the door behind him. "Excuse me," he said, "but would you all mind stepping into the office for a moment. Monsieur Giraud has arranged a surprise for you." So saying, he crossed to the tapestry and removed it, showing the door. I felt to make sure my pistol was available and, reassured, sat back in the chair. I took Tania's hand while the others watched and waited for Fritz to open the door. As they filed in, Fritz seated them, and I spoke to Tania.

"Where is Anna?"

"She went to St. Étienne with me. She was feeling much better."

"Well, I don't understand why you didn't leave a note with Danielle. We were both very much concerned."

"But, Jules," she said, "I did leave a note. Out on the coffee table outside where she always serves me breakfast." She smiled and patted my hand. "I know all about it. When we returned and discovered the house locked up, I went to your place and found Danielle, and she told me the whole story. It had been chilly yesterday morning, and she thought I'd rather take my coffee inside, so she never went out to the table. Come," she said, standing, "the others are waiting. What's the surprise?"

I shrugged nonchalantly. "If I tell you, it won't be."

Fritz had me seated to the left of Lupa's desk, facing the others. Tania sat opposite me, and next to her, Paul, then Henri and Georges, with Henri on my far right. Fritz exited. No one spoke. In another moment, the door opened again, and Fritz asked me to help him bring in the cases of beer. I went back out to the apartment, and he closed the door behind me.

Lupa came out from down the hall and motioned me quiet with his finger to his lips. "The table?" he whispered.

"Only that small depression—looks like a spiderweb."

He smiled. "Yes, I thought I remembered that. Satisfactory. It closes the circle. I'll be right in."

Fritz and I took the beer inside and set it behind the desk. I sat again and Fritz walked out, leaving the door ajar.

"What's the surprise, Jules?" asked Paul. "The tension is killing me."

"Tension rarely kills," said Lupa, appearing in the doorway.

"People kill." He closed the door behind him. The lock clicked into place.

They were all on their feet. Lupa ignored the commotion, crossed to his desk, and sat. As he reached for a beer, the noise died down.

"What's the meaning of this, Jules?" asked Georges, but they all shared the sentiment.

"Please, please," Lupa admonished, opening his beer and pouring, "let us be civilized. I've arranged it, through Monsieur Giraud, that all of you would be here tonight. Last week, one of your friends was killed in our presence. The police have witlessly concluded that I am the guilty party, and this is not the case. The purpose of this little meeting will be to expose the killer, which is one of you."

"But you're the killer," Henri exploded.

"No, sir," Lupa replied. "I am not. Most assuredly."

"I won't stay," said Paul.

"Oh, but you will. The door is locked. Besides, what have you to fear? If you are innocent, no harm will come to you. If not, well . . ."

"I'll tell you what we have to fear," said Georges. "We have *you* to fear. Last week you killed Marcel and that inspector. Tonight you might kill any one, or all, of us."

"Oh, tut, sir." He looked around. "Please, all of you, relax. Would any of you care for more beer? I nearly forgot to have it brought in."

There were no takers.

He leaned back. "Now, then, where to begin? We may as well get at the facts." He sighed, then drank, then began.

"The rumors you have heard about this case being an

international affair are perfectly true. Since I will be long gone, and certainly in no danger from any of you, I can afford to tell you this. I am an Allied spy."

He paused for the words to sink in. "Now, then. I was sent here just after the war broke out to try and learn the identity of one of Europe's most dangerous minds and, having done so, to stop him.

"I'd been having no luck until last Wednesday, when Monsieur Giraud fortuitously invited me to your weekly gathering. The person I sought undoubtedly knew me, since I'd chased him through Eastern Europe for several months preceding my move here to Valence. He kept eluding me precisely because he knew who I was, though I changed my identity and papers in every location. Finally, when I learned that he'd come to Valence, I decided to come here as a worker, find a job, and stay hidden and anonymous until he acted or made a mistake. However, nothing happened for so long that I began to fear he'd left.

"In desperation, I accepted Monsieur Giraud's offer to be seen in public. My luck was extraordinary. The man I was trailing was at that first gathering. Of course, not knowing him put me at a distinct disadvantage, which he decided to capitalize on immediately. He tried to kill me."

He paused to look at the assemblage. "Of course, you're probably wondering why he chose that drastic method when, in the past, he'd simply run."

"I was wondering that," said Paul, dryly.

"The answer is, as my father would say, elementary. He had to remain in Valence until some other job was completed. Last week I learned and yesterday it was verified that

that job was the destruction of the St. Etienne Arsenal. So he had to stay, and he had to elude me. When, by mistake, he killed Monsieur Routier, he put me hot on his trail again, for the first time in nine months.

"I resolved not to lose him again, and I haven't. Killing Routier was an act of panic, provoked by seeing me. If he'd kept calm and done nothing, he would have succeeded in his mission at no danger to himself. Monsieur Routier, by the way, since he is dead and the knowledge can do no harm, was himself an agent of the French government, seeking this same man."

A murmur ran like a current through my friends—"What? Marcel? *C'est impossible!*"

Lupa continued, oblivious to their reactions. "I surmise that at the time of his death, Routier's cover was still intact, which means that his espionage connections were still unknown, even to his murderer. That much by way of prologue. Are you sure none of you will have more beer?"

I looked at the faces of my friends. The men all were wary, and Tania was furious.

"I'd like another beer," said Henri.

"What about Monsieur Giraud, here?" Tania said. "Why is he helping you? Is he a spy, too?"

Lupa looked at me. "Him? Don't be silly."

"Then why are you helping him?" Paul asked me.

"Marcel was my best friend," I answered. "After he was killed last week, Monsieur Lupa took me into his confidence, and I believe him. I want to see Marcel's killer punished, even if it is one of you."

"It is," interjected Lupa. "What you don't seem to realize

is that any of you could have sat in the seat I vacated last week. Whoever sat in that seat would have been poisoned."

They eyed one another, a hint of suspicion finally creeping into an expression or two. Henri sipped his beer and wiped sweat from his brow; Paul leaned with his elbows on his knees; and Georges stiffly crossed one leg over the other. Tania was still angry.

"All right," Lupa went on, "so my first problem was who to suspect, and at first that, too, seemed simple. Suspect Monsieur Lavoie, since he's the only one who was not in Valence during the time I was chasing someone in the East. I saw the flaw in that almost immediately and cursed myself thoroughly, I assure you. The murderer, assassin—call him what you will—rarely did his own work. I hadn't been chasing him all that time, but rather his agents. I checked with another of my contacts on that point, and he agreed. So I had two scores to settle with this man: he'd tried to kill me, and he'd made me look a fool."

"Then how did he recognize you right away?" asked Paul again.

"Photographs." He drank some beer. "You're listening carefully. That's a good sign."

"You still look a fool to me," said Henri.

Lupa nodded. "Perhaps, but let's go on. I was left suspecting everyone, so I had to eliminate. Madame Chessal." He looked at Tania and she met his gaze. "I'm sorry I suspected you for so long, but it began when I entered Monsieur Giraud's house last week. I'm sure you didn't realize it—indeed, you couldn't have—but you, in your close observation of me, changed your position as I did all evening, even after the murder. If I crossed my legs, you crossed your legs, and so on. And so you gave away your interest in me. At the time, I had no idea what could cause that interest, except of course the obvious."

He opened his desk drawer and pulled from it the photograph I had delivered earlier. "Only yesterday did I learn that I closely resemble your eldest son."

"Damn," I said, "he does." Tania's son had a mustache and was much smaller than Lupa, but the face was very similar.

"Where did you get that picture? Jules"—she turned to me, her mouth taut—"did you have anything to do with this?"

Lupa butted in before I could speak. "Monsieur Giraud is more your friend than you know, madame. The point is, do I or do I not remind you of your son?"

Tania, still fuming, lowered her eyes. "Yes," she said coldly. "I saw it then."

"Precisely. And you've been piqued at me ever since because your son is in the war, at the front, and I'm not." He leaned slightly toward her. "Be assured, madame, that I too am fighting this war." He continued. "Later, when you came to question me about missing the funeral, I was on my guard and so was perhaps unnecessarily abrupt. I now apologize. And I thank you for your help with Anna's wounds."

The others looked quizzically at us.

"Last Sunday," Lupa went on, "another attempt was made on my life, this time wounding a woman I was with and barely missing an associate. I have been extremely fortunate, I admit. At the time, I thought it possible that my pursuer had hired an assassin and wanted to be sure he'd done his work.

Shortly afterward, I realized that that was folly. A hired assassin would have killed me. No, my man was terrified, and was acting as his own agent. In the past, he'd avoided being the center of suspicion because he'd avoided direct action. Now, once he'd acted, the inexorable pull of events would lead to his downfall.

"So I finally rejected you as a suspect, and happily. Monsieur Giraud was most unwilling to believe you guilty."

"Thank you for that," she said to me.

"Monsieur Pulis," he said, turning his gaze full upon Henri. "I'm surprised the police haven't arrested you, since you've acted the most like a guilty man. When the police discovered cyanide in your house, you panicked, and have been on edge since that time. Monsieur Pulis's son is a photographer," he explained to the others, "and cyanide—Prussic acid—is used in the developing process." He wagged a finger at Henri. "You should have immediately offered yourself for thorough investigation, but instead you were terrified that the police would arrest you because you are not French, and you tried to hide, distorting some facts, lying about others. You should never have lied about seeing Inspector Chatelet, for example. That made me suspicious of you, and it had nothing to do with your nationality. Last Wednesday, you were blatantly unhappy to see me. Actually, that worked in your favor, since the man I sought would never have shown himself so openly. I finally discounted you when I couldn't see any possible way that you could bring destruction to St. Etienne, despite your deliveries there. Though it wasn't crucial, I also found it difficult to believe that the man I sought had a high-strung wife and six children to support.

"That leaves the bachelors. To be fair, let's start with Monsieur Giraud. He convinced me of his innocence by his actions late the night of the murder, and if that wasn't enough, Routier's recommendation was."

This last, of course, was nonsense, but I kept my silence.

Lupa half turned in his seat and reached for another beer. After opening it, he stared at the two men sitting directly opposite him. Paul shifted nervously in his chair. Georges lit a cigarette.

"Mr. Anser. I was loath to suspect you originally because you share my country of citizenship. But consider these facts: you were sitting next to me last week, and were in the best position of anyone else in the room to simply switch glasses with me during the commotion over Monsieur Lavoie's hand. You are an amateur geologist and as such have access to, or have had access to, cyanide. You are a crack shot, by your own admission. You are not French and you live in St. Etienne. The circumstantial evidence against you is, therefore, impressive. On the other hand, last week I sent one of my own men to try and 'cross over' with your help. He was most persuasive and most subtle, and came away convinced that you had no idea what he was hinting at." Lupa turned to me. "That, Jules, was the mysterious man you saw with Mr. Anser when you went to St. Etienne." He went on. "Still, that you refused my man by no means completely cleared you. You might have recognized my ploy and acted accordingly. No, it wasn't until I discovered that Monsieur Lavoie was the man whom I sought, and that wasn't until yesterday afternoon, that I listed those circumstantial facts concerning you as coincidental."

All eyes were on Georges. He sat calmly, smoking.

"I take it," he said to Lupa, "that you are accusing me?"
"Yes."

Georges chuckled mirthlessly. "This is rather tedious, you know."

Lupa shared the grim humor. "I don't really find it so, but perhaps you would like another beer. It may be your last for a long time. Still no? Well. It was admirable the way you arranged to be out of town during most of this week. It did serve to divert attention from you for a time—long enough for you to go about your special tasks.

"Let's begin with last Wednesday. By the way, consenting to be a regular guest was an admirable choice of covers. Whether it had begun by design or by coincidence, you wasted no time in recognizing the value of this particular group to your ends. They were a singularly respectable, though eccentric, group of citizens. Your presence among them established your bona fides in an especially effective manner. To the rest of the community, your status as newcomer—and hence a natural object of rumor and suspicion—was substantially mitigated. Then, too, among a group with so many foreign connections, you stand out as passably French. It was a fine decision on your part."

"Thank you," said Georges sarcastically.

"Don't mention it. But to continue, when you saw me enter Monsieur Giraud's sitting room last Wednesday, you immediately recognized me, as I've said. Perhaps my small deductions that evening were a misplaced show of bravado, but in any event you wasted no time, since an agent like yourself is always prepared. I am, too. While the others were preparing for their toast, you slipped from your pocket a

mercury fulmonade cap which you'd earlier procured, no
doubt, by prying it from the back of a bullet. Much smaller
than a *petite pois*, it was an admirable weapon. You placed it
on the table and brought your beer bottle down on it, causing it to explode and cutting yourself. The explosion, by the
way, left a small but recognizable mark on the table.

"You then excused yourself to dress the wound and, passing my seat by the door, took advantage of everyone's being
grouped around the spilled beer, as you knew we would be,
to drop the poison—stolen from Monsieur Pulis, I assume—
into my glass. You didn't even have to break your stride.

"When you returned and found that Routier had inad-
vertently returned to my seat and drunk the poison intended
for me, your panic increased. Please correct me where I may
be wrong."

Georges sat quite still. "Every word is wrong."

Lupa smiled. "Of course. I didn't suppose I'd catch you
with that. Still, there were other endeavors to which you
were committed, and you had a timetable to follow, so the
next day you had to go to St. Etienne and deliver an exces-
sive amount of gauze to the arsenal. That you entered and
met Monsieur Ponty was incidental. What was not incidental
was his comment on learning of your trade. He said, 'I hope
we can keep your deliveries small.' Monsieur Giraud, here,
has an admirable memory and repeated back to me your
conversation with Ponty. That comment aroused my suspicion, and I fell on it like a hungry dog.

"From that moment on, you were my prime suspect. But
you had worked well and left few clues. When Chatelet was
killed last Friday night, I was tempted to cross you off, but

then my associate in St. Etienne had reported that he'd been followed back to Valence, and by his description, I assumed it had been you. The man who followed my agent, by the way, did not have a limp, but we'll get to that. So, in fact, you hadn't gone south on business, but had remained here, hoping to get a chance to kill me.

"Chatelet, with a bit of terrible luck for both of you, ran into you on the street as he interrogated Pulis Friday night. Worse yet, Pulis then introduced you to the inspector. Of course, between Henri's being your friend and Pulis's deep suspicion of me, it never crossed his mind that your presence was questionable."

Henri, his face red now and dripping with sweat, looked wide-eyed from Georges to Lupa. Again and again he seemed to be trying to swallow, but the dryness of his mouth wouldn't allow it. Remembering his beer, he sucked at it like a man dying of thirst.

Lupa pressed on. "Still, Chatelet presented you with an immediate danger. He wouldn't even have to suspect you of anything. Merely his knowledge that you were in Valence would have condemned you."

Georges still smirked. "Why, exactly, would that be?"

"Because in questioning the other suspects, possibly including myself, that fact would have come out. In other words, you were not in St. Etienne where you were believed to be. In fact, you had followed my man to Valence."

"Fascinating," Georges said.

"Not really," Lupa answered. "So Chatelet presented too great a risk, and you did away with him.

"On Sunday, you followed me to the woods where I was

to have had lunch. When you saw your opportunity, you fired three times but, luckily for me, you missed. That must have been particularly galling for you. When Monsieur Giraud and I gave chase, you ran, and you escaped."

Lupa leaned back and pulled the bell for Fritz. "That," he explained, "was my signal for Fritz to get Magiot and his men."

"That'll be the end of you, then," said Georges levelly.

Lupa drank his beer. "We'll see. Well, to get on with it, yesterday you succeeded in your primary mission, which was to blow up the arsenal. To do that, you used one of your agents—I'd be curious to know how you recruited the janitor, since all the employees there had 'Top Secret' clearance, but that's another question. Reasoning told me what he had done. My man in St. Etienne, who'd been watching the place all day, noted that the smokestacks had stopped functioning about an hour before the explosion. Shortly afterward, the janitor had left the building.

"What he had done was to enter the boiler room in the fifteen or twenty minutes when, according to Ponty, everyone in the building, including the men stoking the boilers, was acting as a 'pack mule.' He opened the doors to the boilers and stuffed them with as much of your excess gauze as he could fit. The boilers are located, or were located, directly adjacent to the ammunition room, and an explosion of the boilers would of course set off the highly unstable dynamite in the next room. The gauze effectively stopped up the pipes, creating intolerable pressure within the boilers. It also stopped their smoking for at least a half hour before the pressure became critical.

"There was your flaw. There is no other explanation for the smoke stopping just prior to the explosion. You thought it would go unnoticed, and for the most part it did. Only my agent there noticed it. Otherwise, it was a brilliant plan. You were having lunch with Messieurs Anser and Giraud while the pressure was building in those boilers. But you should have stayed with directing your agents. When you act on your own, you make mistakes. My agent, you see, swears that he can identify the man who was following him. He didn't know it was you, but now we'll give him a chance to say if it was. Watkins!"

Watkins seemed to magically appear out of the wall as he pushed aside the tapestry and stepped out of the tunnel. Everyone gaped.

"How many secret entrances does this place have?" Tania asked.

"None anymore. You've seen them all." He turned to Watkins. "Is he here?"

"Yes, sir."

"Kindly point him out."

He pointed at Lavoie. I reached inside my jacket to be near my pistol just in case it would be needed.

"That's all very clever," said Georges. "It's a neat little theory, with the minor drawback of being completely false. You can't prove a word of what you've said."

Henri cleared his throat. "You were here . . . I mean we did meet you, the inspector and I . . ."

Georges smiled at his friend. "I never denied it, Henri. The point never came up, did it?"

Henri, confused, leaned back in his chair.

"Monsieur Lavoie is right," Lupa said to the group. "I could have paid this man to come in here and identify him. There is no proof. And so, now, I'm going to ask him to do something which will undoubtedly demonstrate his innocence."

"Certainly," Georges said, his smile ice. "I'd be glad to end this farce."

"Well, then. The man who trailed Monsieur Watkins, here, had no limp. I contend that you have no limp but rather a substantial lifter in your left shoe. You can easily demonstrate which of us is right by taking off your shoes."

"This is ridiculous!"

Lupa shrugged, then leaned back in his chair. "Go on, Georges," Paul urged. "Let's get to the bottom of this."

Georges looked around at each of the group, and the sentiment was unanimous. I saw his glance at the tapestry from behind which Watkins had entered, and my grip tightened on my pistol.

Finally, he came to some conclusion and reached down as if to undo his shoelaces. How he did it I don't know, but by some sleight of hand, he reached into his jacket and came out with a pistol which he trained on Lupa, the hammer cocked.

"All right, now," he said calmly, "no one is to move."

But I had already moved. My pistol was out. "Georges, drop it!"

He turned toward me and fired at the instant I did. I was hit under the left collarbone, and spun backward and to the floor. Tania screamed and crossed over to me. I felt her place my head in her lap.

"Jules, are you all right? Jules."

I couldn't speak, and the room began to spin before me.

There was a pounding from outside, then the sound of a door opening and boots on a wooden floor. I opened my eyes and tried to focus them. It looked as though Magiot and his men had entered. They gathered around Georges, who lay prostrate on the floor.

Lupa spoke, the words coming to me as though through wads of cotton or gauze. "There's your man, inspector. He's dead."

I passed out.

wouldn't be at all surprised if he were to return to the fray before long. There was no talk of marriage to Anna, though I gathered that they were together still. Watkins is back in England, presumably with his olives.

There were several strange offshoots from the Lavoie case. Paul and Henri both decided to enlist, and even though Henri was rejected, it brought forever to an end our beer gatherings. And Tania . . .

Tania lost her second son three months ago, and for a time she fell back into thinking herself old and useless. Her eldest son, the one resembling Lupa, received a furlough and came home to comfort her. After that, she recovered a bit and began nursing me daily. Fritz complained about constantly having a woman in the house, but I was happy to have her. One day, she entered my bedroom early in the morning and threw back the curtains, letting the sun stream in. She was beaming.

"Monsieur Giraud?"

"*Oui.*"

She came and sat by the bed.

"I'm afraid my fears of approaching old age have been groundless."

"That's what I've always said, my dear."

"But more than you know, love. To avoid a scandal, I'm afraid you're going to have to marry me." Our laughter shook the house.

And so, six weeks ago, Madame Chessal became Madame Giraud. We hope our child will be a girl.

After Tania and Danielle moved in, Fritz eventually moved out, but there were no hard feelings. He'd been in touch with

· 17 ·

It is now August, and we are entering our second year of war. I write in the sitting room, propped on the settee with a pad before me. It looks as though Lupa was right. The war may drag on for a long time.

Miraculously, the bullet did no major damage, and the doctor estimates that I'll be completely recovered in another month. In all, it's been a pleasant recovery period. I've used the time to write this report of my last case. Really nothing formal, of course. Something to read in my advancing years and with which to recall the way it all had been.

Lupa has written twice, from Corsica. After that last Wednesday meeting, Magiot took him in for questioning, but released him after Tania went in and spoke for him. Within twenty-four hours he was gone, taking Anna with him. His first letter was written obviously in the first flush of relaxation. He said it was his first vacation in four years. The second letter, however, showed signs of restlessness, and I

Lupa constantly, and planned to go home to Switzerland for a while, and then on to Corsica. Since they'd begun the rationing of food in earnest, losing Fritz wasn't the tragedy it might have been.

Perhaps strangest of all, Magiot has been around to visit. He's apologized several times for his earlier opinion of me. He'd no idea I was, in his words, "such a man of action." He's even gone so far as to say I deserve my retirement.

We had the Pulises and the Magiots around for dinner the other night, and Magiot said he'd heard I was to receive the *Legion d'Honneur*.

Though I had by now earned his respect, he couldn't resist the opportunity to get in one last dig.

"Do you really think, Jules," he asked, "that the medal is for your efforts in the Lupa business? It seems a rather grand gesture for what was really a rather insignificant episode. Compared to the larger war, I mean."

"My dear Jacques, there's no doubt in my mind that the recognition is for what I do best."

"And that is?"

"I'll tell you what that is," Henri said. "It's for making the finest damned beer in France."

"Hear, hear," said my wife.

I beamed all around and raised my glass with my good arm. "I'll drink to that," I said proudly. And so we all did.

JOHN LESCROART, the *New York Times* best-selling author of such novels as *The Mercy Rule, The 13th Juror, Nothing But the Truth,* and *The Hearing,* lives with his family in northern California.